Brief Encounters

Phillipa Ashley
Nell Dixon
Elizabeth Hanbury

E-scape Press Ltd, England.

First published in 2011 by E-scape Press Ltd.

This is a work of fiction. All of the characters, organisations, and events portrayed in this novel are either products of the author's imagination or are used fictitiously.

Brief Encounters. Copyright ©2011 Phillipa Ashley, Nell Dixon, Elizabeth Hanbury.

ISBN: 978-0-9561191-6-2

British Library Cataloguing-in-Publication Data.

A CIP catalogue record for this book is available from the British Library.

1

Published by E-scape Press Ltd, England.

www.escapewithabook.com

Contents

Nell Dixon

Nell Dixon is a Black Country author. Married to the same man for over twenty-five years, she has three daughters, a tank of tropical fish and a cactus called Spike. Winner of the RNA's prestigious Romance Prize in 2007 and 2010, she writes warm-hearted contemporary romance for a number of publishers in the US and the UK.

Booklist:

Little Black Dress

Just Look at Me Now 9780755354375

Crystal Clear 0755354354

Animal Instincts 0755345207

Blue Remembered Heels 0755345185

Samhain Press

Marrying Max

Things To Do

Freya's Bower

His Darling Nurse

Astraea Press

Making Waves

Dangerous to Know

For David, aka Mr Nell, sometimes a brief encounter can turn into the love of your life.

Plus One Guest

"You have to be kidding?" Diana eyed Lucy with suspicion as Lucy moved her office chair away from her desk and replaced it with a large, blue inflatable exercise ball.

"Nope, I need to lose these last two pounds by Saturday and desperate times call for desperate measures." Lucy sat precariously on the ball, adjusting her position until she could reach her keyboard.

"You've finally flipped." Diana grinned, and shook her head in mock despair.

"It's supposed to tone your tum and bum whilst burning calories and improving your posture."

"Blimey, does it work?"

Lucy smiled back. "No idea, but I have to do something so that I can get in my dress for the wedding."

"Have you done anything about finding someone to go with you? The invitation is for 'plus one guest'."

Lucy knew what Diana meant. Since her dear, conniving, boyfriend-stealing cousin Shannon was actually marrying Lucy's unfaithful, rat-bastard, ex-boyfriend, finding a suitable man to accompany her to the wedding had been at the top of Lucy's to-do list. So far all her options had failed.

"No joy. Sam from the downstairs office was going to go but now he's loved up with the girl from the sandwich shop, and he thinks she'd be jealous." Lucy sighed and wobbled on her exercise ball.

"Hey Harry, what are you doing on Saturday?" Diana called out to their boss as he ambled out of his office towards them.

He stopped and pushed his glasses back from the bridge of his nose, a confused expression on his narrow face.

"Is this a trick question?"

Lucy frowned at Diana, who blithely ignored her.

"Lucy needs a man to go with her to her cousin's wedding on Saturday. There'll be champagne."

"Di, Harry doesn't want to spend his Saturday watching some strangers getting married, followed by a boring do with a load of my aged rellies line dancing to 'Achy, Breaky Heart'." Lucy knew her face had turned crimson. She'd worked for Harry for three years and, while he was a lovely guy, he was just, well, a bit clueless really. His jacket cuffs were frayed, he was always a little late for everything and although he was only about five years older than Lucy, he never seemed to have any idea about the latest films or music.

Diana continued to address Harry as though Lucy wasn't there. "Think of all the times she's stayed late and done extra work for you. She always makes sure the plant in your office gets watered and she buys your favourite coffee for the kitchen."

"Um, yes, Lucy is a very much-valued colleague." A faint trace of colour appeared on Harry's cheekbones and he shifted uncomfortably.

"Harry, really it's fine." Lucy glared at Diana.

He turned his attention to Lucy. "As it happens I don't have anything special to do on Saturday." He cleared his throat with a small cough. "So, erm, if you would like some company at your cousin's wedding, I'd be happy to oblige."

Lucy overbalanced on her ball and had to grab at the edge of her desk to haul herself upright. She had to be hearing things or else she could have sworn that Harry had actually agreed with her friend's stupid idea.

"That's great, it'll really help Lucy out, won't it Luce?" Diana looked like the cat that had got the cream.

"Okay, well if you give me all the details, I'll pick you up on Saturday." Harry smiled gently before adding, "Oh, and please use a chair to sit on in the office Lucy; health and safety, you know."

"I could kill you!" Lucy hissed as soon as he'd returned to his office safely out of earshot. "What were you thinking? Harry is a nice guy but he's the nerdiest man on the planet! He probably won't even remember to pick me up!"

"You needed a man and you're running out of time. It was either Harry or having that cow, Shannon, giving you pitying looks all through the reception because you hadn't got a date. Besides, Harry is okay. He's a bit David Tennantish-looking I've always thought."

Lucy bit her tongue opting not to point out that Diana had never once mentioned David Tennant and Harry together in the same sentence before. At least now she had her 'plus guest', even if it was only Harry.

By eleven-thirty on the morning of the wedding Lucy had been to the hairdressers, had a manicure and pedicure and squeezed herself into a designer dress that had cost her more than a week's salary. Harry was late. Not that she'd given him the right time to pick her up anyway. She'd deliberately told him to collect her half an hour earlier than necessary expecting him to be unpunctual. She'd also emphasised the need to dress to impress. If he turned up in his favourite dog-eared dark green jacket, she would die.

Finally, the knock came at the door of her flat. Lucy took a deep breath, picked up her wrap and hoped Harry wouldn't be wearing his usual battered brown suede boots.

"I know, I'm a bit late and I'm sorry." Harry coloured slightly and looked apologetic as she opened the door.

Lucy closed her mouth with a snap and forced a smile. He had certainly made an effort. His suit probably had been fashionable once, about ten years ago, his glasses with the slightly wonky frames were gone and he'd swapped his suede boots for dark coloured shoes.

"Have you got gel in your hair?" she asked.

"Um, my brother said it was what everyone did." He fidgeted as if embarrassed by the admission. "You look really beautiful, Luce."

Harry had nice hazel eyes, now he wasn't hiding behind his glasses. Her heart melted a little. He'd given up his Saturday and gone to all this trouble just to do her a favour, and she was behaving like an ungrateful moo.

"It looks great." Her smile widened.

He looked relieved by her comment. She locked the door of her flat and followed him to his pea green VW Beetle.

He slowed the car as they approached the small group of guests standing outside the picture postcard-perfect church. Lucy's stomach started to churn. She'd only seen Rory and Shannon twice since Rory had sent the text. That brief message had smashed Lucy's romantic daydream that he might be 'The One,' to smithereens. She had never really got on very well with Shannon ever since they'd been toddlers. Shannon was everything Lucy wasn't: tall, slim with a generous bust, a complexion that always appeared to be lightly tanned and access to fabulous clothes thanks to her step-father's fashion store.

Harry found a parking space next to the church, jumped out of the car and raced round to open her door. He extended his hand to help her out.

She got out quickly, pretending a need to brush down her skirt, the frisson of electricity from his touch leaving her slightly flustered.

"Thank you. Do I look okay?" She tucked the designer bag she'd bought from eBay under her arm.

His dark hazel eyes locked on hers. "You always look lovely, Lucy."

Her breath caught in her throat. She had to have imagined the glimpse of emotion she thought she'd caught in his gaze when he'd looked at her. Then her mother called her name.

"Lucy! Oh, I'm so glad you decided to come. I know how difficult this must be for you seeing Shannon and Rory together." Her mother caught her hands in hers, breaking the spell.

"Mum, this is Harry, he's a friend from work." Lucy decided not to tell her mother that Harry was her boss otherwise it might open a whole floodgate of questions.

As Harry shook her mother's hand, Lucy noticed her mum giving him a quick appraising glance.

"Impressive hat, Mum." She deftly steered her mother towards the entrance of the church with Harry falling into step beside them. The long curled navy feathers on her mother's hat bobbed about in the light breeze like the wings of a demented Muppet.

"Your Aunty Viv helped me choose it."

Harry exchanged a glance with Lucy and she bit back a giggle, his expression seeming to reflect her own thoughts about her aunt Viv's sartorial expertise. They filed into the church and took their seats on the bride's side near the front. Rory was seated at the end of the front pew sandwiched between his best man and a huge stand of peach roses.

She'd thought it would hurt to see him dressed in a new suit, waiting for Shannon to make her entrance. She waited for the familiar empty feeling of despair to rush through her. To her surprise she discovered her only emotion instead was mild curiosity to see how he looked on his wedding day. Before she could avert her gaze, Rory turned his head and spotted her. He flashed a faint smile of acknowledgement before giving Harry a more searching look.

There was a small commotion as Shannon's mother and stepfather scurried into their places in the church. Lucy didn't have much time to take in Aunt Viv's tangerine and black ensemble before the organist struck up with the familiar strains of the Wedding March signifying the arrival of the bride.

The service was mercifully brief, although punctuated by the sound of Aunt Viv sniffling into a tissue as the happy couple made their vows. The slew of little bridesmaids in peach satin were relatively well behaved and no one had written 'help' on the soles of Rory's shoes.

Lucy braced herself ready for the photography session and the inevitable questions about her 'plus one' guest as they all followed the bridal party outside. She was soon swamped by a group of elderly relatives all keen to ask her how she was, and who she had brought with her to the wedding. Over her great-aunt Emily's shoulder she saw Harry undergoing an interrogation by her mother. He had his hands thrust in his trouser pockets and the feathers on the top of her mother's hat were waggling frantically as she spoke. Lucy had to force herself to feign an interest in the family news of great-uncle Eric's prostate surgery and her other cousin, Louisa's new job in Australia.

A few minutes later when the photographer called them all to pose for the group pictures, Harry rejoined her wearing a thoughtful expression. Lucy resolved not to think about what her mother might have said to him and dutifully pasted a smile on her face for the photographer. She skilfully managed to dodge talking to Shannon and Rory as they made their way to the bridal limousine ready to lead the way to the country house where a glass of sherry and the wedding breakfast awaited them.

Lucy climbed into the front seat of Harry's car and put on her seatbelt. "Just the reception to get through now. We don't have to stay too long after the speeches if you'd rather get away." She plucked some stray pieces of confetti from her skirt.

"I hadn't realised that you used to date the groom," Harry said as he inserted the car key into the ignition.

Her face heated. Thank you, Mother. "Yes, I did. Then he met Shannon, and well, that was that." She tried to keep her tone light and prayed Harry would simply hurry up and start the car without probing any further.

Her colour heightened further as he turned to look at her. "So that was why Diana was so keen to enrol me as your escort for today?"

"Yes, I didn't want to turn up on my own like some lonely, sad loser who couldn't get a date. It would have been too humiliating. I would have given the whole thing a miss but then my mother would have been convinced I was dying of a broken heart, and Shannon and Rory would...oh, what does it matter?" She couldn't bring herself to meet Harry's gaze.

When he didn't immediately reply she stole a quick peep at his face. She couldn't read his expression.

"It clearly matters to you, Lucy." He tucked a stray lock of her hair back behind her ear with a gentle finger.

Her mouth dried at the tenderness in his eyes and the reply she'd intended to make died on her lips. For one brief, wonderful second she thought he was about to kiss her, but to her disappointment he turned away and started the engine.

"We'd better get a move on or we'll be late."

Lucy hardly noticed the scenery as they drove to the reception. She'd actually wanted to kiss Harry. Harry, her boss, the man she'd worked with for over three years. Harry of the frayed cuffs and untidy hair. Dear Lord, all this and she hadn't even had any champagne yet.

She drank three of the tiny glasses of sherry being handed out by the waitresses in quick succession. She would have tried for a fourth except Harry steered her away from the bar area. It was hard to decide which was more unsettling, the thought of having to shake hands and congratulate Shannon and Rory as she passed along the receiving line or that she'd wanted Harry to kiss her when they'd been in the car.

"I do like the young man who's come with you," her mother whispered in her ear as Lucy mentally braced herself to enter the room where the food was to be served.

"He's just a friend from work, Mum." Lucy whispered back. She knew what her mother was like. If Lucy didn't put her straight she'd be putting two and two together and making twenty-six.

"Pity."

Lucy was suddenly inclined to agree with her. Maybe the sherry was stronger than she'd thought. She followed her mother towards the receiving line where Aunt Viv and Shannon's stepfather, Ted were first to shake her hand, kiss her cheek and thank her for coming.

"I was so pleased you came, Lucy. Especially after everything that happened, I'm glad you weren't too upset." Aunt Viv's perfume made Lucy's nose twitch as the older woman embraced her.

"Well, if Shannon doesn't seem to mind having our Lucy's cast-offs why would it bother Lucy?"

Lucy cringed as she heard her mother's voice slapping her aunt back into place and Shannon's tanned shoulders stiffened above the ruffled and sparkling bodice of her wedding dress. Fortunately Harry stepped in to kiss Aunt Viv's cheek and introduce himself. He also somehow managed to slip his arm around Lucy's waist before Shannon could greet her.

"You must introduce me to the beautiful bride, Lucy." He smiled at Shannon as if he hadn't heard Lucy's mother's comment. Lucy was so startled by his cool diplomacy she stammered her way through the introduction.

Shannon had no choice but to greet Harry politely, but if looks could kill then Lucy would have been on her way to the morgue. With Harry gently but firmly steering her along, she only exchanged the briefest of handshakes with Rory before she found herself escorted away from the wedding party.

"Are you all right?" he asked, his arm still around her waist. Lucy decided she quite liked the feel of it there, comforting and supporting her.

"Yes, I'm fine. Have you ever considered a job in the diplomatic corps?" She was surprised she'd managed to make a joke even though her pulse was still racing and her legs were a little shaky.

"We'd better find our seats." He led her to the seating plan.

Shannon had allocated them seats well away from the top table where they were surrounded by people Lucy didn't know, some of whom turned out to be work colleagues of Rory's. She was so wound up from the stress of the receiving line she thought she wouldn't be able to eat anything, but the food proved delicious and Harry was an entertaining companion. He seemed to have an easy knack of being able to engage people in conversation and even had everyone laughing at some of his jokes.

By the time the champagne was poured for the toasts and the speeches had begun, Lucy was totally relaxed. The tension knot between her shoulders had unravelled and it didn't seem to matter any more that Rory was talking about his beautiful bride. She was only aware that Harry was seated next to her, his hand resting tenderly on hers.

Finally the speeches were done and the champagne drunk. The music started and Rory and Shannon took to the small dance floor for the first dance. Lucy felt strangely detached from the scene. In the weeks leading up to the wedding she'd pictured this moment, thinking it would be unbearably painful. Now it was here, she only felt numb and disinterested, as if she were watching it on a movie screen, and she had no personal connection with the couple on the dance floor.

The music changed and other couples got up and joined Rory and Shannon.

"Would you like to dance?"

Harry's question jolted her out of her reverie. "I didn't know you could dance."

"Only this kind of dancing." He led her onto the dance floor where the other couples were slowly circling round to a popular soft rock ballad.

As Harry took her into his arms Lucy's heart rate increased and she barely registered Shannon and Rory staring at her as she floated by. The dance floor shrank until she was only aware of the man holding her in his arms, their feet moving automatically to the beat of the music. She longed to snuggle closer to him, to rest her cheek on his lapel. When the music changed to a more upbeat number she felt bereft as he released her.

Whatever else she might have expected at Shannon's wedding she hadn't imagined herself falling for Harry. Or that he might be interested in her, or was he? She was so confused, it was hard to think straight. Perhaps some cooler air would give her some perspective.

"If you'll excuse me, I think I need some fresh air." Lucy forced herself to walk away.

Her heels crunched across the gravel and she paused at a small stone balustrade overlooking the rose gardens of the country house hosting the reception. Faint strains of the disco floated out to her as she sucked in deep breaths of the rose-perfumed air.

"Lucy?"

She turned at the sound of Harry's voice.

"Why did you offer to come with me?" Suddenly it was important to know why he'd agreed to Diana's absurd request.

He moved a few steps to stand next to her, a small frown furrowing his brow.

"If I tell you, then promise me you won't let it affect our working relationship." He plucked an innocent leaf from one of the nearby bushes, twisting it between his fingers.

Lucy swallowed. "I promise."

He shot her a brief glance before scowling at the remains of the leaf. "I've wanted to ask you out for ages, but I'm your boss and you always seemed to have a busy social life and I'm not too great at the whole dating thing." The words came out in a clumsy rush as a dull red stain crept along his jaw.

Tears prickled the backs of Lucy's eyes.

"I didn't know." Her words came out as a whisper.

"When Di suggested I come to this do with you I thought maybe it was my chance to see if you might be interested in me. Then your mother told me about Rory." He plucked another leaf from the bush.

"I couldn't give a toss about Rory." Lucy reached out to take the remnants of the crushed leaves from Harry's fingers.

She saw his eyes light up at her words.

"Really?"

She nodded and he stared at her, an incredulous look in his eyes.

Trembling slightly, she placed her hands on the tops of his arms. "I'm not the fastest person on the uptake, Harry, but all day I..."

She didn't manage to finish her sentence before his lips closed on hers and she lost herself in his kiss. It was every bit as good as she'd thought it would be, and then some.

"...I've been wanting to kiss you." Harry murmured as they broke apart.

She smiled her answer back at him as he dipped his head to claim her lips once more.

"Just a friend, my foot!" She heard her mother exclaim as she lost herself again in Harry's kiss.

The End.

A Weekend In Venice

Disappointment washed over Kay, as grey and flat as the waters of the lagoon. La Serenissima was before her, partly shrouded in misty drizzle. No, this wasn't what she'd signed up for on her European weekend break. Scaffolding, blue plastic sheets and rain that seemed to seep through the water-resistant material of her peach jacket had not been listed as attractions in the travel agent's brochure.

She clutched the handle of her holdall a little tighter as the water taxi slowed on its approach to the jetty. Perhaps it had been a mistake to come here after all, and especially to have come alone. She should have listened to her mother and her friends in the office when they had warned her not to expect too much from her journey. Only her Grandpa Joe had encouraged her, and this whole mad idea had been his suggestion in the first place.

There was the usual scramble as her fellow passengers made their way off the ferry and onto the jetty. Kay followed at the back, her balance a little unsteadied by the rocking motion of the boat on the water. Once safely ashore, she delved into her bag for the map and directions to the hotel.

A large droplet of water found its way under her coat collar and trickled down the back of her neck as she studied the instructions. So much for spring sunshine, glamour and romance - not that she wanted romance. She refolded the map and tucked it back inside her bag. At least the bright pink walls of the hotel should be easy to spot amongst the misty watery grey of the other buildings. With luck she wouldn't need to try out her basic Italian cribbed from a guidebook she'd picked up in a charity shop.

Kay pulled her collar closer to her neck and set off in search of her hotel. The musty smell of the surrounding water enveloped her and the damp crept into her bones as she carefully picked her way through the side alleys checking her route as she went. For a split second she thought she saw him, the familiar back of his head, his short black hair plastered against his skull by the rain. Then logic kicked in and leaden sadness settled in her stomach as she realised it was impossible, she would never see Laurence again.

As she rounded the final corner she breathed a sigh of relief. There was her hotel, exactly like the picture inside her bag. Like its neighbours it was an old building, but the brochure had promised a modern and comfortable interior.

An hour later with her bag unpacked and her wet coat drying in the bathroom, Kay sat in the lobby with a small dark coffee in a china cup. She leaned back into the stiff leather backrest of her chair and the ache in her temples began to ease as she sipped her coffee and took in her surroundings. Warmed by the heat of the drink, and with the fragrance of the freshly ground beans scenting the air, some of the tension knots between her shoulder blades began to ease away.

Perhaps Grandpa Joe had been right. She had needed to get away from home and go somewhere new. She'd turned down her friend's offer of a girly holiday in Spain and her mother's plan of a week in Torquay in favour of this weekend in Venice. Her Grandpa had been the only person who'd appeared to understand her need to do something on her own. His tales of Venice when he'd been a younger man had fired her with a desire to go and see the city for herself. Here there would be no memories of the past to torment her, and maybe, just maybe, the city would somehow manage to jolt her back to life.

She closed her eyes as she remembered the snippet of hushed conversation between her mother and her grandfather after she'd announced her plans of travelling to Italy. They'd thought she was safely out of earshot.

"You shouldn't be encouraging her, Dad, she's still frail. It's only been a couple of months since she came out of hospital."

"And getting stronger every day. She needs to do this. She needs to get away from everyone watching her all the time, treating her like a child."

Kay had heard her Grandpa sigh and then the soft rustle of fabric where she had guessed he had hugged her mother. "You have to let her do this, and it's only for a long weekend. What harm can it do?"

Her mother's response had been inaudible, and with her cheeks burning, Kay had scrambled to escape from the house to sit in the car ready for her mother to take them home.

She took another sip of coffee, savouring the bitter taste. It was one of the few things that held any taste since she'd lost Laurence. She even managed a small bite from one of the two tiny almond biscotti that had accompanied her drink. Through the window the soft May rain had almost ceased. The lobby was quiet, another couple sat at a nearby table studying a map whilst they chatted, and at the elegant polished wood desk an elderly man was checking in. No one looked at her.

Kay collected her jacket and map. There were still a couple of hours of daylight left now that the rain had stopped and she only had a few days to see the sights. The air was cooler outside the hotel and Kay snuggled deeper into her coat. She tightened the belt around her waist to prevent it from flapping open in the light breeze, trying not to dwell on why it was too big for her these days. She decided to head for St Mark's Square as it was only a few minutes' walk away. Then, if the rain started again, or if her legs hurt too much, she wouldn't have too far to go to get back to the hotel.

As she stepped out from beneath a stone archway the sheer size of the square overwhelmed her. She'd seen pictures, of course, and Grandpa Joe had told her how large it was. Even so her breath caught at the back of her throat as she slowly turned to take in the space. The rain hadn't deterred the visitors and despite the puddles which lay on the stone paving reflecting the grey sky, there were still lots of people there.

The pale stone colonnaded archways surrounded her on three sides whilst the majestic beauty of St Mark's church dominated the far end. She made her way through the pigeons which flew around gobbling up crumbs from the sandwiches and crisps scattered or discarded by the visitors. She walked towards the terracotta bricked tower of the Campanile di San Marco. A short queue of people were waiting to take the elevator to the top to see the view. Her feet moving automatically, Kay joined the end of the line.

A few minutes later she stood at the top of the tower looking out over the square and the surrounding buildings. The breeze was stronger and colder now she was higher. It whipped her short brown bob across her face so she had to raise her hand to sweep her hair from her eyes. Her engagement ring slid to her knuckle as she moved her hand, loosened by the weight she'd lost whilst she'd been in hospital. Tears filled her eyes, blurring her vision momentarily before she blinked them back.

Kay blundered her way through the throng of people and into the lift for the return journey back down to the square. Her hands trembled as she thrust them into the pockets of her jacket and prayed no one in the elevator would notice her reddened eyes and shaking fingers.

Out in the vast square, she decided to make her way back to the hotel. She still felt shaken from the rush of memories that had swept through her when her ring had twisted. Memories of Laurence, the accident and all the broken dreams of a future that could no longer be hers, threatened to overwhelm her. Even here, everything was grey, lifeless and flat.

She should have died along with Laurence, there was nothing for her anymore.

She blundered along without heeding her surroundings for a while before she realised she'd taken a wrong turn. The narrow alleyways and tall stone buildings were unfamiliar. She tugged her map from her bag and tried to work out her route. After a brief moment of panic, she thought she'd spotted where she'd gone wrong. The late afternoon light was already fading as she rounded a corner to discover a small row of shops, the windows glowing enticingly in the gloom.

One shop in particular caught her eye. The display was of small Murano glass objects, the fine crystals winking and twinkling against a background of deep blue velvet like stars in the night sky. Amphoras, goblets, bells, rosarys and beads sparkled under the halogen display lights. Mesmerised, Kay stared at the display, admiring the colours and craftsmanship of the pieces.

Hesitantly, she pushed open the shop door, which had a delicate etching of a unicorn's head in the glass, and went inside. The interior of the shop was tiny, display cases covered the walls, each one backed with the same deep blue velvet that had been used in the window display and brightly lit to show the colours of the glassware.

"Buonasera Signora? May I help you?"

Kay startled at the unexpected sound of the man's voice cutting across her thoughts. She turned round to see a man of around her age standing behind a tiny desk in the back corner of the shop.

"Scusi, I think I make you jump." He smiled at her and Kay sucked in a breath. Even surrounded as he was by lovely objects, he was easily the most beautiful thing in the shop.

"Yes, I'm sorry I was miles away. These things are so lovely." Her voice sounded harsh in her ears, her accent English and dull, next to the rich sonorous tones of the shopkeeper.

The man stepped forward into the light. "Thank you; they are the work of my family. Have you been yet to the island of Murano and seen how these are made?"

Kay swallowed, she could feel colour mounting in her cheeks as she dropped her gaze, trying not to stare at his velvet brown eyes, high cheekbones and the thick dark curls that tumbled onto his collar.

"No, I only arrived today. I'm hoping to go tomorrow as I only have the weekend to see everything. I've just been to the top of the Campanile." She knew she was gabbling.

To her relief he didn't laugh. "Then you must visit Murano before you go home. Are you here with a party?"

"No, I'm travelling alone." Once more, tears rose at the backs of her eyes.

"My name is Roberto, my family has made glass at Murano for many years. I am looking after the shop here today for my sister, Rosa."

Kay fumbled for a tissue and dabbed swiftly at her eyes. Grateful that he hadn't commented on her tears, she found the voice to introduce herself.

"I'm Kay. I'm from England. I work in a solicitor's office."

Roberto held out his hand to shake hers. "Hello, Kay from England."

A tingle passed through her skin as he shook hands with her, the tone of his reply to her odd introduction reflected by the gentle smile on his lips. Kay found herself smiling back at him, her hand still resting loosely in his.

"You are staying near here?" As he released her fingers, Kay felt almost bereft at the loss of contact. The strength of the emotion surprised her; it had been so long since she'd felt anything.

She nodded, "The Splendid. I was on my way back there and got a bit lost. That's when I saw your shop."

"It's not far away. You have a map?"

She tugged the map from her bag. Roberto spread it out on the top of the small desk which served as a counter. "You are here." He made a small mark with a pen to show the location of the shop, "And your hotel is here." He made another mark nearby.

"Thank you." Kay refolded her map and looked up at him once more.

His dark eyes locked with hers.

She dampened her lips with the tip of her tongue. "I should be going." She didn't want to. She willed her feet to move, but she remained rooted to the spot.

Roberto picked up a leaflet from the desk. "Tomorrow, when you go to Murano, visit here and give my name. Look for the sign of the unicorn, my family crest. I promise you will not be disappointed. People say there is magic in our glass."

Kay took the thin sheet of paper and tucked it in her bag next to her map. "I will. Thank you."

He smiled at her once more and Kay made her way out of the shop and into the now dark alley. She wasn't sure what it was about the chance encounter with Roberto that had stirred her senses so much. As she walked back to her hotel she went over the brief conversation in her head. It had been innocuous enough, he was probably just a talented salesman trying to direct tourist traffic to his family's business.

She shook her head. No, if he had wanted to sell something she could have bought something from the shop. It had been when he had looked deep into her eyes, almost as if he could see the recent pain and loss written on her soul. Then his words, "I promise you will not be disappointed. People say there is magic in our glass."

After a peaceful and delicious dinner, Kay retired to her room. The leaflet Roberto had given her rested on the dresser next to her map. The hotel receptionist had provided a vaporetto schedule and explained how to visit Roberto's glass factory.

"Always haggle, Signora, over the prices in the showroom if an expensive piece takes your fancy."

As she turned off her lamp ready for sleep Kay wondered if she was being foolish by going to the showroom. After all, there were lots of glass blowing factories on Murano, all linked by small bridges. She could go to any of them, she didn't have to just go to Roberto's. It wasn't as if he would be there or she would be likely to see him again. She closed her eyes and ignored the tiny spear of disappointment in her chest at that last thought.

The next morning, after breakfast, Kay set off to catch the vaporetto to take her on the short journey across the water to Murano. Overnight the weather had changed and the sky was a clear pearlescent blue, brightening the waters of the lagoon and imbuing the view with a lightness that had been missing yesterday. Kay's spirits rose accordingly and for the first time since leaving hospital she realised she felt excited.

Roberto's factory and showroom wasn't far from the jetty where the vaporetto set her down. As she crossed one of the ancient stone bridges towards the showroom her pulse picked up speed and she couldn't help hoping that maybe she would see Roberto again.

Once inside the building with the Unicorn sign above the door, she somehow found herself with a small group touring the factory. Surrounded by strangers, she watched the whole process, step by masterful step. The glowing red of the molten liquid, the gold leaf being applied to the jewellery and the skill of the craftsmen as they fashioned the delicately beautiful objects, held an almost magical fascination for her.

Perhaps that was what Roberto had meant when he had said, "there is magic in our glass". Kay wandered through into the showroom, considering this. Maybe he was just a skilful salesman giving her the patter after all.

Her shoulders drooped along with her spirits as she surveyed the beautiful glassware for sale in the showroom. She selected a small photo frame as a gift for her mother and took it to the sales counter, deciding she would forget about the meeting with Roberto.

"You would like this wrapped, Signora?" The elderly man at the desk had a voice more heavily accented than Roberto's but Kay fancied there was a family resemblance in the man's dark eyes.

"Yes, thank you. It's a gift for my mother."

The man smiled and wrapped the frame carefully in layers of tissue paper and bubble wrap. He secured it in a small gold bag with a paper seal bearing the same unicorn's head she'd seen on the leaflet and the door of the shop near the hotel.

"How did you find us, Signora?" The man asked as she handed over her money to pay.

"I met someone called Roberto yesterday and he told me to come here." Kay wished she could recall the words. She hadn't intended to mention Roberto's name even though he'd told her to say he'd sent her.

The elderly man smiled. "My grandson. You must be Kay, from England."

Kay stared at him. Roberto had told his family that she would come to their shop?

"I have something here for you." Roberto's grandfather bent and picked up a small parcel from under the counter. "It is a small gift, a memento." He passed the package to Kay.

"Oh, but I couldn't, I..." Her face bloomed crimson with embarrassment at the unexpected gift.

Roberto's grandfather picked up the parcel and placed it in her hand. "My English is not quite as good as my grandson but this is for you. Only you."

Stammering her thanks, Kay took Roberto's gift and placed it in her bag along with the picture frame before hurrying out of the shop. Flustered by the unexpected turn of events, she wandered around until she stumbled on a small coffee shop. She took a seat at one of the outside tables and ordered a cappuccino.

After a few sips she started to feel less agitated and slipped Roberto's gift out of her bag onto the table. Her fingers trembled as she carefully unwrapped the delicate object inside the layers of tissue. To her surprise she found a small pastel-pink glass heart threaded on a grey leather cord. As she held it in her hand she noticed traces of gold in the pink glass as it warmed against her skin, glittering like tiny veins in the morning sunshine. A folded piece of paper accompanied the gift.

She wrapped the pendant back inside its protective layers before opening the note. Her heart skipped a beat and tears prickled at the back of her eyes as she read.

'Dear Kay,

Please accept this small gift. I told you yesterday that there is magic in our glass. I hope one day your heart will be as whole and healed as the heart you found in this parcel, and the sadness which haunts your beautiful eyes will be gone forever. Wear it when you feel alone and let its magic take away your sorrow.

Roberto'

Kay swallowed and reopened her gift. The pink glass heart lay on its cushion of paper. She stroked it gently with the tip of her finger and again felt gentle warmth emanate from the glass before she picked it up and slipped it around her neck.

A calm sense of peace filled her as she finished her coffee, feeling the unaccustomed weight of the pendant against the skin at the base of her throat. She paid for her drink and set off back towards Roberto's showroom, intending to at least leave a thank you note for his gift.

Yet she didn't seem to be able to retrace her steps. She paused near one of the bridges wondering if it was the same one she had crossed only a few minutes earlier. Maybe she had somehow doubled back on herself. Cursing herself under her breath for her inability to find her way just a few yards without her map, she saw she was in a small square outside a beautiful and surprisingly large ancient church. Magnificent arches dominated the exterior drawing her notice. A few trees provided shade and the waters of the canal slapped at the jetty nearby.

Kay saw the door stood open and a woman appeared to be taking donations. She handed over some euros and entered the church. Once inside, her eyes adjusted to the candle lit gloom of the interior. She walked slowly forwards, her gaze drawn upwards towards the golden dome with its blue mural of the blessed virgin. The glass heart around her neck seemed to warm even further as she drank in the sights around her.

Incense fragranced the air, colours assaulted her vision and the blood pounded in her veins. Her legs trembling, Kay sank down onto one of the pews. Automatically she slipped her fingers around the small glass heart at her throat.

"I'm so sorry." Her words were inaudible. She closed her eyes. She was alive; her life had been spared for a reason. So many people loved her, cared about her. Her mother, her grandfather and now, she clutched the pendant, a stranger who had wanted to make her happy once more.

She waited for a moment until she felt calm once again and, after placing some money in the donations box she lit a candle for Laurence. As she stepped away, ready to leave the church and return to the square, she was aware of someone in the shadows by the door. A man with the face of an angel who had given her back her heart.

Kay smiled, her first proper smile since the accident and walked forward towards the sunlight streaming in from the square. And Roberto.

The End.

Elizabeth Hanbury

Elizabeth Hanbury was a finalist for the 2008 Joan Hessayon Award, and is a member of the Romantic Novelists' Association and the Historical Novel Society.

Her Regency novels The Paradise Will and Ice Angel are published by Robert Hale Ltd.

Her collection of Regency short stories, Midsummer Eve at Rookery End, is published by E-scape Press Ltd.

To find out more, visit Elizabeth's web site at
www.elizabethhanbury.com

Miss Pattingham Requests

"I must have misheard you, Philip. Why should I go to Kensington at any time and especially at four o'clock this afternoon? A gruesome place, populated by demireps and gossiping old ladies."

Gyles Beaufort, who had glanced up only to address this comment to his secretary, returned to the papers on his desk. As was usual at this time in the morning he sat in the study of his London residence, Beaufort House. A tall man with penetrating eyes, Mr. Beaufort's air of distinction owed little to his dress which was often careless but today was dishevelled. His coat and cravat had been discarded and his shirt lay open at the neck. A heavy frown marred his brow. Dark smudges under his eyes spoke eloquently of sleepless nights. His raven-black hair looked as if he had been out in a high wind, so often had his fingers been pushed through it. His mouth was unsmiling, his jaw set in an uncompromising fashion.

The Beaufort House library had not escaped the pervading sense of gloom either: the window blinds had been drawn to keep out any spring sunshine that dared to enter and even the spaniel lying near Beaufort's feet rested his head on his paws in a disconsolate fashion.

Philip Thorpe had been Mr. Beaufort's secretary for three years. Given Beaufort's reputation and being himself a man of unimpeachable morals, Philip had expected the appointment to prove a trial. He had been proved wrong. Mr. Beaufort made no unreasonable demands, his requests were generally accompanied by one of his attractive smiles and he was never disagreeably high in the instep.

In short, Philip had found it impossible to dislike Mr. Beaufort. It therefore pained him to see his employer toiling under
such misery now. Philip, giving his employer an assessing look,
saw there had been no improvement in his mood or appearance.
Indeed there had been none for three weeks and during that time
the stricken empty look in Mr. Beaufort's eyes had only intensi-
fied.

But a proud man like Gyles Beaufort refused to put personal
turmoil before duty. He had continued with this daily ritual,
although Philip suspected that he spent much of the time brooding over recent events and scouring the newspapers rather than
working. In truth, Gyles did not need to attend to such matters
himself – as the son of a duke's daughter with a large fortune,
an unassailable position in society and a very efficient secretary,
Gyles Beaufort could idle his days away in any manner he chose.

In the past he had done so. Philip knew that Beaufort's
behaviour as a younger man had often been wild; unsurprising,
perhaps, when one considered how he had been toadied all his
life. As well as the advantages of wealth, status, good looks and
charm, Gyles Beaufort was an acknowledged leader of the ton, a
crack shot and an excellent whip. Every door had been thrown
open to him and, even when he reached the age of twenty eight
and began to take his responsibilities more seriously, he continued
to enjoy those pleasures available to a single man.

If the rumours were to be believed, he had enjoyed many
liaisons with beautiful women who were, in the common par-
lance, up to snuff, but never with a view to marriage. He made
no promises on that score. Matchmaking mamas and eligible
damsels alike had laid siege to him for ten years in the hope of
engaging his interest. None had succeeded until two months ago
when in one of those implausible twists of fate, Gyles Beaufort
had fallen for a pretty but penniless girl he had met by chance
in Bond Street. He had then undergone the kind of epiphany
that happens to men of rakish tendencies when they fall in love.
A whirlwind courtship had followed and when at last he had
convinced Miss Merryn Ward of the depths of his passion, his
determination to forsake his previous lifestyle and to put her

happiness above all things, she had accepted his offer. An announcement of their engagement had appeared in the Morning Post the following day.

Despite the speed of their romance, Philip had never seen a couple more suited or more in love. An orphan from a genteel family rather than of aristocratic stock, Miss Merryn Ward was an intelligent, quietly elegant, sensitive woman. She was not a great beauty and lacked the assurance of a lady born to inhabit the ton, but she possessed an indefinable inner luminance which impressed everyone who met her.

She had certainly touched Gyles Beaufort's soul, bringing out the very best in him. If whispers about their disparity in fortune and status, or Beaufort's previous reputation with women ever reached Miss Ward's ears, she gave no sign of it. They radiated happiness and their match seemed one made in heaven until it had all ended abruptly three weeks ago when Mr. Beaufort had received a letter.

Philip had no idea what was in the missive his employer received – how dearly would he love to know! - but he had been present when Beaufort had read it and witnessed the powerful effect it had exerted. After a long silence, an ashen-faced Mr. Beaufort had hastily scribbled a note and told Philip to deliver it to the lodgings where Miss Ward lived with a distant aunt. But Miss Ward was not there, nor had her aunt any notion of where she had gone. She had collected her belongings earlier, declared she was leaving London and vanished.

In the days that followed, Philip and Mr. Beaufort had searched high and low for Merryn Ward. They had instigated numerous enquiries and placed notices in the newspapers, but so far their efforts had been in vain. She seemed to have disappeared from the face of the earth, leaving Gyles Beaufort a shattered man.

And now, when Beaufort's agony seemed most acute, Philip had to break the news that his presence was required in Kensington.

He shuffled his feet. "I'm sorry Sir,' he began, holding up the lavender-scented sheet of paper in his hand, 'but this letter is from Miss Pattingham, your old governess. She requests that you have tea with her at four o'clock today at her house in Kensington."

"Miss Pattingham *requests*?"

"The invitation is more in the form of a summons," admitted Philip.

"I see." Gyles passed a weary hand over his eyes. "Explain to me why the deuce I should oblige Miss Pattingham with a visit at all?"

"Well, you have supported her financially for many years – I understood she was a kind and generous influence on your childhood and as you always thought of her with affection, you wanted to ensure she could live out her old age in comfort."

"That is true, but I'm not a child anymore and I see no need to answer her command. Particularly now."

"I understand Sir, but in the letter she mentions her delicate health. Apparently her heart is not strong and she says would be glad of this opportunity to see you."

Frowning, Mr. Beaufort looked up at last. "You are of the opinion I should humour Miss Pattingham?"

"It would be a kind gesture."

A smile touched Gyles' mouth. "Ever the chivalrous knight, eh? Your thoughtfulness does you credit."

Philip coloured faintly at this praise. "I simply think your visit would prove of comfort to a frail old lady."

Gyles nodded, sighed and leaned his broad shoulders against the back of his chair. "I have not seen Miss Pattingham for years. We have exchanged the occasional letter of course – she has always been grateful for my support because she had no family other than a widowed sister – but I have no notion of how she goes on in general. Like most governesses, she was a disciplinarian. She was, however, a fair one and more affectionate towards me than my mother ever was."

"She does not sound at all like my governess."

"Oh?"

"No indeed! Miss Shaw was cross between Attila the Hun, Lucretia Borgia and Genghis Khan,' replied Philip, giving an involuntary shudder. 'My brother and I were terrified of her. She was about eight feet tall with a booming voice, beetling brows and an iron grip. If I never see her again, it would be too soon!"

"Good God, she sounds appalling," agreed his employer, a rare gleam of amusement in his eyes. "Miss Pattingham was not quite so intimidating. Apart from a sharp tongue and a nasty habit of making me eat boiled eggs, she was pleasant enough. Shrewd, too – she knew exactly how to protect me from my father's wrath. I wonder if she is still as sharp as a pin."

Phillip studied the letter again. "Her note is a little rambling in places, but the handwriting is clear and the message clearer still – she expects you at her house today."

Gyles groaned. "Paying social calls is the last thing on my mind."

"No, Sir, but if Miss Pattingham is ill, it would be wise to humour her and if you do not go now you might regret it."

"Oh very well," he replied, after a long pause, "but I warn you, Philip, if Miss Pattingham turns out to be completely dotty as well as bordering on a physical wreck, I shall make my excuses before she brings out the tea. And I will not, under any circumstances, be obliged to eat boiled eggs at four o'clock in the afternoon."

***

Gyles pulled up his curricle outside the address in Kensington village at the appointed time. His restless gaze scanned the property. It was a neat little house with nothing to distinguish it from the rest, other than the display of spring flowers in the window and the highly polished brass knocker. This must be the place; trust Miss Pattingham to be fastidious about such matters.

Several curtains had twitched as he drove down the street and he knew his visit was being carefully observed. At any other time, this would have amused him. Indeed spending an hour with Miss Pattingham would not have bothered him unduly. He would not have sought her out, but equally he would have been willing to do his duty by taking tea with an old family servant, or inviting her to Beaufort House.

Now he chafed at being away from his task. Finding Merryn was an all-consuming necessity. He ached for her and thought of nothing else night or day, and when he allowed himself to dwell on the dreadful things that might have befallen her he feared he might go mad.

If Merryn had been at his side he might even have looked forward to this visit. In the short time he had known her, Merryn's generous spirit had put his arrogance and habitual ennui to shame. Visiting a lonely old governess was the sort of thing she would have insisted upon and he would have done it with good grace because the most humdrum activity became a pleasure in her company.

This bitter reflection made him recollect once more what he had lost.

Gritting his teeth, he handed the reins of his team to his groom, ordered him to keep them moving and jumped down from the carriage. Best get this interview over with quickly so that he could return to Beaufort House and see if there had been any news.

His tug on the brass pull at the side of the front door set a bell pealing in the depths of the house. Almost at once the door opened to reveal a diminutive figure dressed in lilac silk with a paisley shawl draped about her shoulders. Miss Violet Pattingham, her silver hair neatly braided, tilted her head to look up into his face and welcomed him with a smile and twinkling blue eyes. She was tiny, reminding him of a little bird, but not as frail looking as he had expected. Her spine was still ramrod straight and she walked without the aid of a stick.

"Master Gyles!" she cried, putting out her hand in greeting. "How good it is to see you! I hoped you would come."

He returned her smile, his large hand engulfing her much smaller one. "Did you doubt it, Patty?" he asked, stepping inside and sweeping off his hat.

She seemed pleased by his use of the affectionate name he had addressed her by when he was a child. "No indeed. I felt sure you would."

"Your invitation left me little choice," he observed in a wry tone.

"I'm aware of that." Her bright gaze ran over him. "My, what a grand gentleman you have become! I hardly recognised you. You make my hallway seem very small."

His lips twitched. "I have grown taller since you last saw me," he admitted, removing his gloves. "You look well."

"Only in parts, Master Gyles," she said, placing his hat and gloves on the hall table. "My rheumatism plagues me on damp days, but I must not complain at my age. And it is so pleasant to have company for tea."

"I am looking forward to it," he said mendaciously. Glancing down the hallway to what he assumed was the parlour door, he took a step towards it, saying, "Shall we go in?"

"A moment please!"

He stopped and looked over his shoulder.

Miss Pattingham was pointing a menacing finger at his polished top boots. "Your boots," she began in an imperious tone, "they might have mud on them. Wipe your feet!"

Gyles Beaufort - rake, nonpareil, leader of the ton, member of White's and the Four Horse Club – stared in astonishment. He was more used to giving orders than receiving them. He was certainly not used to being told to wipe his feet! He opened his mouth, then recalled Philip's warning about Miss Pattingham's poor health and closed it again. Feeling eight years old once more, he gave a rueful smile and returned to wipe his feet meekly on the rug by the front door.

Miss Pattingham nodded her approval. "Very good. Now, let us go through - everything is ready."

Gyles, eying Miss Pattingham's retreating diminutive figure with misgiving, followed her down the hallway. She did not appear to be dotty and seemed remarkably sprightly for a lady with

a weak heart. Resigning himself to a tedious half hour of incon-
sequential chatter and fervently hoping there would be no boiled
eggs waiting for him, he walked towards the parlour.

***

Miss Pattingham's parlour resembled its owner: small and
neat with nothing out of place. There were a few pieces of
shabby but highly polished furniture, including a small table,
a mahogany side board, a dark blue sofa and two armchairs. A
collection of miniature portraits hung on the wall above the fire
and a clock ticked merrily away on the mantelpiece. The parlour
looked out onto the street, affording anyone who sat in the armchair nearest the window an excellent view. Gyles could imagine
Miss Pattingham sitting there to observe passers-by and visitors
to her neighbours' houses.

He had assumed the room to be empty so when a sound like
a sharp intake of breath reached his ears, he turned to see where
it had come from.

When he did, he too gave an audible gasp and muttered an
oath of astonishment.

There, in the other armchair, sat Miss Merryn Ward.

She was staring at him, her extraordinary hazel eyes as round
as saucers in her heart-shaped face, her complexion as pale as the
wall behind her. Clearly she was as surprised to see him as he
was to see her. Shaken to his soul, for a full minute he could only
stare at her in silence while a profusion of emotions jostled in his
breast.

"Ah, so you have noticed my other guest," Miss Pattingham
was saying. "May I present Miss Merryn Ward, Master Gyles?"

"We have already met."

From a long way off, Gyles heard himself voice this laughably
inadequate reply. He could not tear his eyes from Merryn's face,
afraid she might disappear again into thin air. His greedy gaze
drank in every detail of her appearance. She was pale and heavy-
eyed, but to him she looked as lovely as ever. Her reddish-brown
hair was dressed in her usual neat but unobtrusive style. She wore
a green pelisse over sprigged muslin dress, both garments being

faded and outmoded and both of which he had been determined to replace just as soon as they were married. He had wanted to see her dressed in the finest fashions his money could buy.

"Have you indeed?" declared his hostess, looking from one to the other. "That is fortunate. It saves me the trouble of making introductions. I suppose you met at one of the ton parties or some such thing. Do take a seat, Gyles – you are so tall you are blocking out the light!"

"M-Miss Pattingham," stammered Merryn, her lip quivering, "I never thought— that is, I did not expect anyone else to be here this afternoon. I must go at once." She half rose out of her chair.

"Don't leave on my account." Gyles sat down on the sofa, only slowly recovering from his shock.

"Oh no, you must not go, my dear!" declared Miss Pattingham roundly. "I rarely have company these days and this is delightful. Merryn has been staying with my sister in Surrey these past three weeks, Gyles."

"I see," he murmured, his gaze fixed on Merryn. "I wish I had known that."

"It was a spur of the moment decision," confessed Miss Ward, unconsciously wringing hands that trembled. "Daisy - Miss Pattingham's sister - was my governess years ago and when I was ... when I was unhappy and desperate to get away from London recently, my thoughts turned to her. She was kind enough to let me stay and has been a great comfort."

"I'm sorry to hear of your distress," said Gyles, giving her a brooding look. "How strange that I, too, have been suffering from low spirits of late."

Merryn's eyes flew to his. "You have?"

"The worst I have ever known."

"My dears, this is melancholy conversation for a fine spring afternoon!" interjected Miss Pattingham. "It is time I brought in the tea tray – my maid has the day off, but she has laid everything out in readiness."

"Let me help," pleaded Merryn.

"Nonsense!" Miss Pattingham waved her to sit down again. "Stay and talk to Gyles – since you two already know each other, there should be no awkwardness. I will return directly."

She went out and a long, awkward silence promptly followed.

It was broken when Gyles cried out in an anguished voice, "Dear God, Merryn, do you know what agonies you have put me through?"

"No less than you deserve," she flung back with a flash of fury.

"I'm relieved you are safe, but why in God's name did you leave?" he pleaded. "*Why?* We were so happy."

"You know why."

"I do not, I swear it."

Tears shimmered in her eyes. "Even now you cannot be truthful," she murmured bitterly, shaking her head. "That pains me more than anything else and makes me wonder how many more lies have fallen from your lips."

"None! I have always been truthful - my love for you would permit nothing less."

He reached for her hand, but she snatched it away. "I suppose you can claim to have told no lies, but your actions have been dishonourable. I was foolish enough to believe you had forsaken your old ways. How naïve to think a rake could change!"

"I don't know what you are talking about," said Gyles. "At least tell me exactly what crime I am supposed to have committed. Or am I not to have the opportunity of defending myself?"

"You would just tell more lies and I cannot bear it." A noise from the hallway made Merryn jump and she added in an urgent whisper, "Shhh, Miss Pattingham's coming back! Daisy told me that her sister's health is not good – that is why she asked me to come to London, to deliver a tonic to her – and I refuse to upset such a dear old lady by arguing in front of her. Whatever our differences, we must humour her while we are here—"

Merryn broke off as the door opened and Miss Pattingham came in, bearing a fully laden tray which she set down on the table. She seemed unaware of the tense atmosphere and declared as she sat down in the chair next to window, "I hope you have been getting along while I have been away. Of course, strictly speaking it's against the proprieties to leave you alone, but Gyles is a gentleman so I have no fear for your virtue, Merryn."

A sound suspiciously like "Pshaw!" emanated from Miss Ward.

Either Miss Pattingham did not hear this or she chose to ignore it. She simply gave another of her bright smiles and held out a plate to her other guest. "Hard boiled egg, Master Gyles?"

***

Merryn watched as his face turned white, then a faint shade of green.

He was regarding the platter with barely disguised horror. His lips clamped together and he shook his dark head resolutely. Really, she thought, even when he was turning green at the thought of eating a boiled egg, which she knew he detested, he was too handsome for words. Her heart had leapt with joy when he had walked in unexpectedly. Foolish! How had she ever believed a girl like she could engage the love of a man like Gyles Beaufort? It was too ridiculous and yet, for a few short weeks, she had allowed herself to believe and it had been the most magical time of her life. That had made her subsequent fall back to reality more painful. Part of her still wanted to believe in him, in the man she had thought he was, but she could not deny the evidence of her own eyes and ears. She blushed at her gullibility; she had been far too trusting.

"Thank you but no," he was saying. "Since leaving the schoolroom, I don't partake of boiled eggs."

Miss Pattingham's face fell. "But I insist!" She pushed the plate closer. "I made them knowing they used to be a favourite of yours. They are very nourishing and I shall be upset if you do not have at least one."

"Really, I cannot—"

"Please, Master Gyles!"

Trapped, Gyles shot a despairing look across the room. Slowly and with great reluctance, he took an egg and ate it, chewing with careful deliberation. It was clearly a ghastly exercise. His gaze held Merryn's and in that moment, the connection she had felt to

him from the instant they had met flared into life. Recalling the
laughter and the love they had shared, she forgot momentarily
how unhappy she was, the pain he had caused her and the dis-
tance between them now. His expression of ludicrous dismay and
the sight of the nonpareil Beau Beaufort being coerced into eating a boiled egg by a petite silver-haired old lady set off a bubble
of laughter in Merryn's throat. She did her best to smother it,
but found it impossible. She giggled and then tried to disguise
it by coughing and instigating a search for her handkerchief.

Miss Pattingham regarded her sympathetically. "Have some
tea, my dear," she said, thrusting a cup in Merryn's direction.
"It will help."

"T-Thank you," gasped Merryn. She dabbed her eyes and
took a sip.

"You're too thin, you know," mused Miss Pattingham, assessing her guest's slim figure. "You need more flesh on your
bones. Pray have some cake."

She carved an enormous piece of seed cake, put in on a china
plate and passed it to Merryn.

"But this is far too much," said Merryn, aghast. "It's more
than I could eat in a week!"

"Nonsense!" avowed Miss Pattingham briskly. "A young girl
like you should have a hearty appetite. Master Gyles has eaten
his egg and you should eat some cake. After all, I had it baked
especially for this afternoon."

"But—"

"Now please don't disappoint me, my dear!"

With her hostess standing before her expectantly, there was
nothing else for it but to comply. Merryn took the plate and
again exchanged glances with the man across the room. There
was an unholy gleam of amusement and understanding in his eyes
as he watched her take a bite.

Merryn hardly contributed to the conversation that followed
as she was too busy with the enormous slice of cake. All the
time she was aware of Gyles' amused gaze on her. The cake,
which was rather dry and full of caraway seeds which Merryn
disliked, did not seem to diminish. The sensation of swallowing

a mixture of sawdust and brick dust was almost succeeded by another coughing fit. She seemed to be eating forever yet the slice appeared no smaller than when she had started. Eventually she pushed the remainder aside. The notion of another morsel made her feel nauseous.

"Excellent! We are all getting along famously," declared Miss Pattingham. She looked at the tray and frowned. "We still have the scones to eat, but oh dear, I seem to have forgotten the apricot jam. My memory is not what it was. It will take me but a moment to fetch it from the kitchen. Do, pray, have some more cake and eggs while I am gone. I'm determined neither of you will leave until everything has been eaten."

She scurried out of the room again and when she was safely out of earshot, Gyles groaned.

"If I have to eat another egg, I can't answer for the consequences!"

Merryn put down her plate and grimaced. "I feel the same about this! If I have to swallow another crumb, I shall be ill."

"I noticed you struggling with it." He looked at Merryn, a brief smile lightening his stern features. "Well, as we're at least agreed not to upset Miss Pattingham, shall we find a way to save both her feelings and our stomachs?"

"How?"

"We must be quick. Do you have a reticule with you?"

Merryn nodded.

"Open it as wide as you can." Before she could realise what he was doing and protest, Gyles picked up the plate of eggs and tipped them unceremoniously into the green velvet reticule she held out.

Merryn stared at the now bulging reticule in horror and then hissed in a furious undertone, "Why did you do that? Surely she will notice!"

"I doubt it, but if you have a better idea, I'm willing to listen."

Merryn had to confess she had not. "But what about the cake?"

"Slightly more difficult, I admit, but I think I may have a solution."

He took two large handkerchiefs from his pocket, wrapped the rest of cake inside them and stuffed one bundle into each pocket of his breeches. When it was done, he folded his arms across his chest and sat there with such an expression of innocence on his face that she was compelled to giggle again. He had always been able to make her laugh.

He watched her, his eyes never wavering from her face. His features softened and then in a flash he leant forward and caught her hands in a hard grasp.

"It's no good, Merryn! Deuce take it, I can't stay silent when I love you so much. Tell me why you broke my heart!" he said hoarsely.

"You broke mine," she whispered, sobering at once. "I saw you. With her."

"Who?"

"That woman. You were with her in Hyde Park and at Fenton's Hotel. Don't deny it!"

"Deny it! I don't even remember—" He stopped, a frown creasing his brow. "When was this exactly?"

"Shortly before I wrote to you to end to our engagement. By chance a few days earlier I was walking with my aunt in the park when I saw you talking to a woman. A very beautiful and elegant woman. You had pulled up your carriage and were strolling with her. You were deep in conversation and did not notice me at all, and I'm ashamed to say that I watched you secretly. I could not help it. I also overheard a little of your conversation – you were arranging to meet her for lunch at Fenton's." The blush that had spread over Merryn's cheeks deepened. "I did not know what to think so I followed you there the next day and, through the window, saw you with her in the coffee room. You were laughing together. Please don't insult me by telling me she is a relative of yours – I know all your female relatives by sight and she is not one of them!' She caught her breath on a wretched sob. 'I assume she is one of your chère-amies."

"She's not a relative. But she's not a chère-amie either." His gaze grew warm as he added gently, "My foolish little love! Do you remember when we went for a drive in Hyde Park and you asked me to stop so you could admire a small dog?"

Her brows drew together. "Yes I remember," she said after a pause. "It was an adorable spaniel being taken for a walk by a maid."

"You said wistfully you had always wanted a dog just like it. I admit I could not see the attraction of the animal just then, but I did not forget the ecstasies you went into and without your knowledge, I went back to the park every day for a week in the hope of seeing the dog and the maid again."

She blinked in amazement. "You did?"

He nodded. "I found them again eventually and by questioning the maid, I discovered the dog was one of several belonging to Isabelle Booth."

"The famous Covent Garden actress?"

"Just so," he confirmed. "I determined to get that little dog for you whatever the cost. Your happiness means everything to me and I wanted to see the delight on your face when I presented the spaniel to you. I sent a note to Isabelle Booth through her maid and asked her to meet me in Hyde Park. At first Isabelle did not want to part with the dog – mainly because she could see how much I wanted it and she was determined to drive a hard bargain. I suggested we share luncheon at Fenton's the following day and discuss terms. After much haggling, a price was agreed and she arranged for the spaniel to be brought round to Beaufort House. I planned to surprise you, but your letter arrived before I could do so."

"Is this true?"

"Certainly."

"Where is the dog?"

"At Beaufort House, probably chewing up my expensive rug."

A heavy silence followed. Merryn pressed her hands to her now hot cheeks. She could not doubt he was telling the truth – the look in his eyes told her that plainly enough and it all sounded alarmingly probable.

"Oh God," she cried, a large tear rolling down her face. "What a fool I've been! I feel utterly stupid and you have every right to be furious. Can you ever forgive me? But I was so sure, so certain ...." Blushing furiously, she hung her head and murmured in a constricted voice, "I'm sorry doubted you, Gyles, but I think I doubted myself more. You see, I could never quite believe you could love someone like me and when I saw you with that beautiful, sophisticated woman all the doubts I had stifled came tumbling out. It seemed to confirm everything I feared. I am a penniless nobody and you are a wealthy leader of the ton; I am an ingénue while you are a man who knows all about seduction - what could I offer you compared to a woman like that?"

He stood up and pulled her into his arms. "Everything!" he declared unsteadily. "I don't want a woman like Isabelle Booth – I want you, Merryn. Now and forever. I don't deserve you, but stay and love me, that's all I ask and in return, I promise to love and honour you and no other until I die." He drew her letter from his pocket and held her a little more tightly. "Now, what should I do with this?"

Dashing away her tears, she smiled up at him. "Put it on the fire."

An answering grin curled his lips and he brought his mouth to hers, kissing her with rough, hungry ardour.

***

Miss Pattingham, returning with the apricot jam shortly afterwards, never enquired about the missing boiled eggs or caraway cake, nor did she comment on Merryn's flushed cheeks or the way Gyles remained at Merryn's side for the rest of their visit.

Sometime later, as they left together in Gyles' carriage, they waved goodbye to Miss Pattingham who was standing in her parlour window.

"Do you think she knew about us?" asked Merryn. "I told Daisy a little about my situation, but I did not mention your name."

"I don't know. Violet Pattingham was always a shrewd woman, but I can't imagine her abilities extend to reuniting estranged couples."

He smiled down at her, making Merryn's heart somersault in her chest. She slipped her hand into his. "Let's invite Miss Pattingham and her sister to the wedding."

In reply he kissed her, a deep, searching kiss that turned her blood to fire.

"Gyles, everyone will be looking at us!" she protested afterwards, breathless.

"In that case, I'll kiss you again."

And he did.

***

In her front parlour, Miss Pattingham sat down at her writing table. She smoothed out an old copy of the Morning Post which was open at the announcements page. A smile curved her mouth as she took a sheet of writing paper from the drawer and began to write:

Dear Daisy,

You will be pleased to know that, just as we hoped and planned, those dear children Merryn and Gyles are reconciled. I believe I shall shortly need to buy a new hat....

The End.

The Virtuous Courtesan

(A Midsummer Eve at Rookery End story)

Author's note

In 2009, I wrote a collection of Regency short stories - Midsummer Eve at Rookery End – published in paperback and e-book by E-scape Press. These proved hugely popular and so, in response to demand, here's another short, sweet and passionate tale from Rookery End.

Those readers familiar with the original Midsummer Eve at Rookery End stories will know the inspiration behind the anthology, but for anyone new to the series, here's a quick primer:

Midsummer Eve at Rookery End came about after I read a book on old English customs and festivals. Midsummer in England was the highlight of the festival year in mediaeval times and continued to be celebrated in various ways, including bonfires, processions and parades. Midsummer Eve and Midsummer Day were also cited as times when particular divinations could be successfully carried out.

Love divinations were the most popular and many were chronicled in old texts. These included girls throwing hemp seed over their shoulder and the baking and eating of a 'dumb cake' on Midsummer Eve, both performed in the hope of seeing the form of their future husband appear. The most widespread love divination was referred to as 'Midsummer Men', where orpines (a native wild flower of the British Isles, Sedum Roseum Crassulaceae, commonly referred to as 'Midsummer Men') were placed in pairs, one representing a man, the other his sweetheart. If the orpine reclined from the other, it indicated that there would be aversion; if the plants inclined towards each other, it indicated love.

Given this history, the idea of a midsummer Regency ball to celebrate these ancient customs, and romance in general, seemed a very appropriate one. Lord and Lady Allingham's country mansion - Rookery End - is an imaginative fusion of my favourite English country houses and gardens. These great estates with their elegant architecture and beautiful gardens provided the perfect stage for the three tales of midsummer love and passion which featured in the original Midsummer Eve at Rookery End collection: Siren's Daughter, Blue Figured Silk and A Scandal at Midnight.

Now, as part of the Brief Encounters anthology, we return to Rookery End and discover just how Lord and Lady Allingham met....

With love,
Elizabeth x
To find out more, visit my web site at
www.elizabethhanbury.com

The Virtuous Courtesan

It was a perfect night for housebreaking.

The moon, sailing across a sky of deepest sapphire, cast a silvery hue over the landscape, the air was heavy with the scent of roses and the sounds of summer drifted on the breeze. Rookery End, the ancestral seat of the Earls of Allingham, stood serene and somnolent under the starlight; no candles burned in the windows. At this hour even the servants would be in their beds and as Leonora peered through the bushes to survey the elegant architecture and gardens before her, she too wished she was asleep. In fact she wished she was anywhere but here and about to embark on the most idiotic venture of her life.

Despite the circumstances she and her father had endured over recent years, creeping around a large country house under cover of darkness was not something she had anticipated doing. How had things come to this? She pushed the thought aside. She had one aim and to be distracted from it could bring disaster.

Besides, it was no use worrying about what could not be altered. Her father had committed a grave error of judgement, but he had done so with good intentions and in a fit of remorse had soon confessed. Of course it was too late by then, yet seeing the desperation in his eyes and knowing he was ill, Leonora had not had the heart to censure him. Instead she had arranged for him to go abroad while she tried to sort out this abominable mess.

The breeches, oversized greatcoat, riding boots and muffler she wore felt strange but deliciously liberating. Earlier, when examining her reflection in the mirror in her room at The Angel Inn, she found the disguise endowed her with a peculiar thrill of anticipation. She looked mysterious, even threatening; a villain indeed, albeit one of slight build. Her long, dark hair was concealed under a battered old tricorn hat. In her left hand she gripped an iron bar. Her paint-stained hands were hidden by gloves and the black muffler covered most of her face. Only her eyes had been visible and they had gleamed back at her, apprehension lurking in their dark blue depths.

Now it was well after midnight and she was within reach of her goal. She made sure her horse Raphael was tethered securely and memorised where she had concealed him. A quick, soundless escape was vital. Raph snorted softly as she stroked his nose, being careful not to disturb the boot blacking she had used to cover his white markings. She was almost ready; only two more details to check. Thrusting her hand into the pocket of her overcoat, she hunted for the small-bladed knife. Still there. In the other pocket, her fingers closed around the smoothly wrought handle of pistol. It was an old-fashioned piece, a relic from her father's youth, and its presence reassured her even though she had no intention of using it.

Leonora exhaled slowly to steady her nerves. She had planned as much as she could – it was time for action. Thank God the fine weather had held! A gloriously sunny afternoon had given way to a perfect midsummer eve and that, together with her research on the layout of the house and her disguise, meant everything was perfectly placed.

All she had to do now was commit the perfect crime.

She ran across the lawn until she reached the shelter of a high yew hedge. After a moment's pause to check there were indeed no candles still burning in the house, she crept closer. A cloud skittered across the moon, leaving just enough light for her to pick her way forward without stumbling. She tiptoed through the neat gardens marking the edge of the terrace and, narrowing her eyes, peered through the gloom until she saw the French doors which opened out from the library, situated at the back of the house.

Her fingers tightened around the iron bar in readiness. Leonora inched forward, flattening herself against the smooth stone wall of the house and praying the sound of breaking glass wouldn't wake the servants. She was almost upon the doors when she saw that one of them was already ajar.

Behind the muffler her mouth fell open in astonishment. She had not expected easy access. Could it be a trap? She had heard tales of owners who didn't bother locking their doors and windows because their dogs roamed free at night, ready to rip any unsuspecting burglar to shreds. Still, the absence of snarling guard dogs made this improbable.

Had another burglar been here before? That too seemed unlikely – there were no signs of forced entry. She frowned, straining her ears to listen for unusual noises.

Nothing.

Only the sounds of a summer night filled the air. How odd. The door must have been left open by one of the servants. Perhaps because Rookery End was situated in the Surrey countryside, locking doors was not as important as it would be in London.

Relief swept through her. Whatever the reason for the door being ajar, it made her task simpler. Now there was no need to smash her way in. Feeling light hearted at this, the first stroke of luck to come her way for months, she dropped the iron bar in a nearby bush and headed for the doors.

It would not take long to remove the painting. Afterwards she could leave Rookery End forever.

***

His head ached like the devil.

Despite the pain throbbing in his temples, Marcus, sixth Earl of Allingham, forced himself to open his eyes. His mouth was as dry as the disgusting sherry his Aunt Maud served up at Christmas. He needed a drink, preferably coffee – the thought of more of the brandy he had imbibed earlier made his stomach lurch. He made a silent vow never to touch another drop of that vintage.

He blinked then winced; even that slight movement set off hammer blows in his skull. God, what a fool he was! At thirty he ought to know it was useless to try and drown one's sorrows – the deuced things always floated to the surface.

Gradually fuller consciousness began to return. The room was in darkness apart from the moonlight shimmering through the windows. The candles Beacham had left on the desk had expired long ago and Marcus judged it to be well past midnight.

He must have fallen asleep. He couldn't blame the butler for leaving him here, fully clothed apart from his cravat and stretched out on the library chaise longue. He recalled being irritable as well as extremely drunk and ordering Beacham out when that venerable retainer, aware of the amount of brandy his master had consumed, had surveyed him with a knowing eye and suggested he should seek out his bed.

With a groan, Marcus pulled himself to a sitting position and clasped his aching head between his hands. He glanced filmily at his surroundings. When his gaze fell on the painting, his mouth twisted in a grim parody of a smile. There, in all her glory and still smiling her damned enigmatic smile, was the reason for his earlier excesses: The Virtuous Courtesan.

The portrait - a full length study of a lady in a low cut, shimmering gold silk gown - was an image of haunting beauty. With her riot of dark ringlets, provocative, slightly mocking smile and slumberous eyes, The Virtuous Courtesan seemed a presence in the room rather a mere painting. Her expression had the ability to draw onlookers' gazes and hold them in rapt contemplation. When a portrait could exercise such fascination over those who saw it, Marcus reflected it was unsurprising that his father, a compulsive collector of art, had desired it so badly. Unfortunately desire had triumphed over reason and Marcus grimaced as he recalled his father's actions. The painting served as constant reminder of his sire's obsession and the legacy it had left his only son to deal with.

His father had died three months ago and while Marcus still felt the pain of his loss, he acknowledged they had never been close. The fifth Earl's passion for art had left no room for other inconveniences such as his wife and son. His wife had died a lonely, painful death while the Earl had been conducting yet another Grand Tour, searching for antiquities to bring back to Rookery End. The teenage Marcus had never forgiven him.

Marcus shook his head, cursing softly. He refused to dwell on the past; he had to look to the future. It was a daunting prospect, but in the years to come and - if he was fortunate enough to ever find a woman who loved him for himself rather than his title and supposed fortune - with the help of his wife, he would turn this beautiful but uninviting house into a home full of laughter and warmth. Any art that could not be enjoyed as part of that home would be sold. As far as he was concerned, art was meant to compliment life, not overshadow it. He had no inclination to follow in his father's footsteps.

But the portrait presented him with a dilemma. It hung over him like Damocles' sword and last night, after several hours of wrestling with the problem, frustration had led to him seeking refuge in the bottle, something he had not done for years. Marcus rubbed his temples to soothe the pain still pulsating there. One thing was certain - getting drunk would not solve the conundrum of The Virtuous Courtesan.

A sound outside made him look around. Instantly alert, he saw that the door was ajar. He must have left it open after strolling in the garden earlier in an attempt to clear his head. The shadowy outline of a figure appeared through the glass and the door began to open.

Someone was about to come in.

It couldn't be one of his servants; only a person with nefarious deeds in mind would be skulking around at this hour. Marcus smiled wolfishly. A turn up with a housebreaker might be just the thing to shuffle off the fog of brandy. He lay back down on the chaise, watching and waiting, every muscle primed for action.

***

Leonora crept into the library with her heart thumping and her breathing fast and shallow. Despite her anticipation, it had been borne in on her during the last few minutes she was not meant for a life of crime. The sooner this was over the better.

Allowing a moment for her eyes to adjust to the deeper gloom, she stepped towards the desk in the centre of the room,

testing each floorboard as she went. No doubt the Earls of Allingham employed the finest craftsmen, but a novice housebreaker
had to be wary of basic mistakes. She wondered how many criminal careers had been brought to an end by creaking floorboards.
Fortunately the English oak beneath her feet made no sound as
she tiptoed forward.

She reached the desk and looked up. A providential shaft
of moonlight illuminated what she had come for. The Virtuous
Courtesan smiled down from her lofty position, the eerie half-
light adding more mystery to her features. On this occasion her
smile appeared welcoming and behind her muffler, Leonora could
not suppress an answering grin – this was proving to be much
more straightforward than she had expected.

With swift, economic movements, she placed a chair near
the wall and stood on it. She took the knife from her pocket and
ran it neatly around the edge of the painting. After extracting
the canvas from its ornate frame with what she hoped was a
minimum of noise, she rolled it up carefully and stowed it in the
leather bag suspended from her belt. She stepped down, replaced
the chair and put the knife back in her pocket before uttering a
deep sigh of relief. Almost done! She turned and had taken two
steps back towards the doors and freedom when her shoulder was
seized in a vice-like grip.

"And what, may I ask, are you about, my fine young buck?"
purred a mellifluous male voice into her ear.

Leonora gasped and almost jumped out of her skin. Recovering quickly, she twisted and squirmed in an attempt to break
away, but that tenacious grip held her fast. She thrust a hand in
her pocket and pulled out the gun, hoping to deter her captor.
He was too knowing and too quick. In a flash he had wrested it
out of her grasp and sent it clattering across the room.

Then she was hauled unceremoniously upright by the collar
of her greatcoat.

"A pistol?" He tutted in the darkness. "Don't you know it's
bad manners to draw a weapon on an unarmed man?"

Leonora aimed a kick in the direction of her captor's shin. It bounced harmlessly off his boot and merely elicited a deep chuckle in response.

"Pray don't rush off," he drawled, "I am eager to hear why you are in my library at the dead of night, stealing one of my paintings. Or perhaps you prefer to explain yourself to the local magistrate?"

She did not reply and tried again to escape. It was an unequal contest. He was like a cat that had caught a mouse by the tail and was waiting until it was exhausted. At one point during the struggle, her legs were thrashing ineffectually in mid air as he lifted her off the ground. The bag at her waist began to drag as if it was full of lead and she felt her strength seeping away.

"Let me go!" she panted at last.

"You're a feisty one," he said, amusement in his voice. He swung her round to face him. "Stop struggling! I'll be damned if I'll hit a slip of a boy even if he is a housebreaker, but I'll be forced to if you won't be still."

Leonora's captor loomed above her, silhouetted against the moonlight. In the uncertain light she could not see his face, but he appeared to be lithe and well-built. The shadow of his shoulders and torso filled her vision. When he shifted his grip to pull her closer, the sudden, unexpected movement caused her to topple against him. A pleasant aroma of sandalwood soap and oak-aged brandy assailed her nostrils, as well as something else – the scent of a virile man. She was not surprised; an older man could not have restrained her so effortlessly during that struggle. She pushed hard against a chest that felt like it had been hewn from solid rock and tried to think. Dear Lord, she was in a fix now! With no immediate prospect of escape, her only chance was to outwit him. Leonora forced herself to relax. The movement was slight, but it did not go unnoticed by her captor and his grip slackened a little.

"Very sensible. Let me look at you." He marched her over to the desk and held her by the arm while he found a tinderbox and lit a branch of candles with his free hand.

A soft glow flooded the room, allowing Leonora to appreciate its beauty. She could see the polished mahogany bookcases which ran along two of the walls; the magnificent red and blue Aubusson carpet; the fine chess set on the table near the fireplace and various paintings, busts, sculptures and objets d'art scattered about the room. The chaise longue near the desk must have been where her captor had concealed himself.

Her eyes flew to his face. Whoever he was, he was a handsome devil. Tall, broad-shouldered and supremely fit, he exuded masculinity. Dark hair sprang from a brow set above a strong, lean countenance and he was studying her with a pair of deep set, piercing grey eyes. She felt a rush of sensation, as if every nerve in her body was tingling in unison. It was a feeling she had never experienced before and she wondered vaguely at it, and why she didn't feel afraid when he was staring at her in that disconcerting way. With a deft twitch, he pushed down the muffler and took off her hat. Her black hair tumbled about her shoulders.

"I thought so," he murmured. "You're not a youth after all. An admirable disguise, but even that coat could not conceal your, er, very attractive assets. Who the deuce are you?"

She returned his intent look. "You said 'your library'."

"What?"

"A moment ago you referred to this room as 'your library'."

"That's because it is."

"Impossible," she declared.

To her surprise, he laughed. Leonora had to admit it was a rich, attractive sound and she couldn't help but notice the tiny lines that fanned out from the corner of his eyes.

"I'm not so drunk that I can't recognise my own library, my engaging little housebreaker. I'm Marcus, Lord Allingham and this is Rookery End. But you must know that – you came here to steal my painting which you did very tidily just now." He pointed to the leather bag. "It's in there."

"Nonsense," said Leonora, giving him a scornful look.

"Are you trying to tell me that I didn't just see you steal it?"

"No, I mean you can't be Lord Allingham. You must be an imposter because I know for certain that Lord Allingham is an older man."

"Ah, you must be referring to my father, the fifth Earl. He died recently."

"Oh!" She digested this and then added in a quieter voice, "Oh. I'm sorry to hear that."

He studied her shocked expression. "You really didn't know, did you? I suppose you assumed stealing from an old man would be easy and that's why you selected Rookery End for your next robbery—"

"No—" she began.

"—a cowardly trick," he continued inexorably, "but then one shouldn't expect honourable behaviour from a thief."

"I'm not!"

"Not a thief?"

"Not exactly."

He raised his brows. "Oh? What are you then?"

"If I explain, will you promise to let me go without involving the magistrate?"

"I promise to consider it." He folded his arms, watching her. "What a delightful puzzle you are! You dress like a rogue and enter my house in the middle of the night. You strip a painting from its frame with the ease of an expert, yet you speak and have the manners of a gently-bred girl, and a beautiful one at that. Why did you only take The Virtuous Courtesan?"

His direct question startled her. "B-Because that was all I came for."

"How considerate! A thief with a conscience, no less. Next you will tell me you planned to give the spoils of your, ah, visit to the poor. Of course, you had no notion it is the most valuable painting in the house."

"I don't expect you to understand," she said, biting her lip.

"Certainly I cannot if you won't explain." His mouth quirked into a sudden smile and he urged in a softer tone, "Come, won't you trust me a little? Instinct tells me you're not an experienced house breaker."

There was so much amused understanding in his manner that Leonora relented. She shook her head. "This is my first and last attempt," she admitted. "I'm not really a burglar at all."

"Then what are you?"

***

Marcus studied the girl before him. Her tumbled hair gleamed like jet in the candlelight. A pair of blue eyes, framed by long lashes, gazed shyly but frankly into his and her mouth was generous and remarkably sensual. As he watched, a riot of conflicting emotions flitted across her face. She was clearly scared to death and doing her utmost to conceal it. He found himself admiring her courage as much as her person, and felt a sudden, violent tug of attraction. Desperate to know more, he prompted again gently, "What are you?"

"I'm an artist."

He lifted an eyebrow. "Indeed? You continue to surprise me. Go on."

"I-I, er, needed this picture" she said, tapping the leather bag.

"This one and no other?"

She nodded.

"Why? Has it cast a spell over you too?"

"No, nothing like that." She flushed to the roots of her hair, but put up her chin, adding, "I can't tell you why."

"My charming rogue, you must to do better than that. I have a particular interest in that painting and I'd like to know why, in your desperation to have it, you were prepared to take such an enormous risk."

"I had no choice."

"Believe me, I can sympathise with that predicament," he replied in a wry voice. "What is your connection to the painting?"

She shrugged. "It's complicated."

"Nevertheless, do me the honour of satisfying my curiosity. It's the least you can do when I've caught you in the act. By the way, how did you plan to get in? The door was open only by chance."

"I brought an iron bar to smash the window."

A muscle at the corner of his mouth twitched. "Enterprising as well as beautiful. There appears to be no end to your talents. Are you in need of money? Is that why you wanted the portrait - to sell it?"

"We - that is my father and I - are always in need of money, but that is not the reason I wanted it back—"

"Wanted it back!' he exclaimed, his gaze riveted on her features. "There seems to be some mistake. The Virtuous Courtesan belongs to me, to my family. Indeed my father pledged an inordinate amount of money to buy it."

Leonora gave a faint moan. "Don't remind me! It makes me feel ill to think of it!"

He stared at her blankly for a long moment. "Perhaps it's the brandy, but I find I am unusually slow this evening. I fail to see why it should it trouble you what my father paid for the painting."

"It concerns me a great deal. You see, it was my father who sold it to him."

***

"Good God," he murmured, visibly shaken. "I should have guessed from the outset this was no ordinary robbery."

"No," she confessed.

He strode over to the fireplace, pushing his fingers through his hair as he went. He laid one arm along the mantelpiece and absently stirred the ashes in the grate with the poker.

"It had to happen, I suppose," he remarked at length. 'Take the wretched thing and be gone! You chose a novel way to regain what is yours, far quicker than involving lawyers. Less expensive too, although I don't understand why your father allowed you to come here in his place. My difficulties will increase when the painting is gone and yet believe it or not you have my gratitude. The estate will remain in debt, but my conscience will be clear."

Astonished, Leonora stared at him. Her head was spinning. She didn't have a clue what he meant, but the important thing was he had told her to go. She should slip away before he changed his mind. She turned and then stopped.

She didn't want to leave yet. She needed to know what was going on and Lord Allingham intrigued her. A short time ago, he had appeared a man in control of his emotions and the situation – now he wore an air of weary resignation. What had she said to bring about such a dramatic change? Clearly she had touched him on the raw. Drawn to him by some unseen, visceral thread, she walked over, reached out and gently touched his shoulder.

"I'm sorry," she murmured. "You obviously love the portrait. The Virtuous Courtesan often has that effect on men. They are enthralled by her."

"Love it? I hate the bloody sight of it," he admitted, with a bitter laugh.

"Y-You do?"

"It reminds me of my father's folly, but you will understand that."

"No I don't." Removing the muffler from round her neck, Leonora walked back to the chaise, sat down and heaved a sigh. "To be honest, Lord Allingham, I haven't the faintest notion what you are talking about. I think it's time we were frank with each other. Agreed?"

He had turned around at her words and now, frowning heavily, joined her on the chaise. "Very well. Let's start with your name."

"Leonora Maddox."

"Then you are indeed the daughter of Captain Henry Maddox - the man who sold The Virtuous Courtesan to my father?"

She nodded. "My father often sells paintings, but this sale was ... different."

"Oh?"

"Before I tell you why, do you know the story behind the portrait?"

"No," he admitted, with a shrug. "My father never told me and I have been too busy arranging matters since his death to find out. All I know is it is extremely valuable."

Leonora swallowed. Taking the canvas out of the leather bag, she unrolled it on the carpet in front of them. "That lady," she began, pointing at the painting, "is Isabella Teresa Roxburgh. Isabella was renowned for her great beauty. When she came to the court of Charles II after his marriage, he grew infatuated with her. It was even said by some that he intended to marry Isabella if his wife, Catherine of Braganza, died during an illness. The Queen recovered, but for several years afterwards Charles considered obtaining a divorce so he could marry Isabella because she consistently refused to become his mistress. Her grace, beauty, intelligence and virtue became legendary and she had many admirers. She refused them all and managed to keep the King's affections while spurning his demands to become his mistress, a difficult path which she managed with dignity and elegance, and which earned her the ironic yet affectionate epithet of The Virtuous Courtesan. Sometime later, Isabella fell in love and eloped with the Duke of Fernhill."

"Did she find happiness with her Duke?"

"She did," said Leonora, glancing up to find the Earl watching her. "And she returned to court eventually and kept her place in the King's affections, a tribute to her quick wits and warm, generous nature."

"A remarkable woman indeed," he observed, his gaze remaining on her rather than the portrait. "The painter has captured not only her beauty, but the essence of her spirit."

Mesmerised, Leonora searched his face. No one had ever looked at her in just that way before and a deep flush crept into her cheeks. For the first time in her life, she felt the urge to confide all her cares and burdens to someone else, and he was a stranger. Her senses were alive, acutely aware of his scent, his warmth, his masculinity, the smile that lurked in his eyes. She wondered if the candlelight had cast a spell over her or if she was suffering from midsummer madness. The thought flashed through her mind that Lord Allingham embodied her ideal. He could have stepped out of her dreams.

Her voice came out in a ragged whisper. "T-The provenance of the original is unclear, but, given its style, is widely believed to have been painted by Sir Peter Lely at about the same time he painted the Windsor Beauties."

"The famous collection of portraits which hung in the Queen's Bedchamber at Windsor?"

She nodded again.

"I see. That explains the high price my father was willing to pay for it."

Leonora flushed crimson. "Yes, but—"

He silenced her by laying a finger gently over her lips. "I don't blame you for wanting the painting back. No doubt you and Captain Maddox have discovered by now that the banker's draft my father made out to cover payment was worthless."

"What do you mean?" she asked, staring.

"Why, simply that my father had been overstretching himself financially for years. Unknown to me, he had mortgaged the estate to feed his obsession. Despite being deep in debt, he could not resist one last acquisition, an item that would be the jewel in the crown of his art collection – The Virtuous Courtesan." He made a sound of frustration. "I only discovered all this after his death and then found myself at the heart of an apparently insoluble conundrum – I could not sell the portrait to help clear the estate's debts, but neither could I keep it. Captain Maddox had received no payment, ergo the transaction was void and the painting still morally and legally belonged to him. Unfortunately, there was no information regarding Captain Maddox among my father's papers. No address, no place of business, nothing, and I've been unable to uncover any trace of him since. That is," he concluded with a grin, "until this evening when his charming daughter-turned-housebreaker crept into my library."

***

"But I know nothing about the banker's draft being worthless," said Leonora, aghast. "When I found out what my father had done, I forbade him from presenting it!"

"How did you come to be here then?" he asked.

Leonora's eyes danced with sudden laughter. "Oh dear, was there ever such a ludicrous tangle? Marcus, I mean, Lord Allingham—"

He caught her hand and kissed it. "Pray do call me Marcus – I like the sound of my name on your lips and this seems hardly the moment for formality."

His tone brought the colour rushing back her cheeks. "Very well," she said, smiling shyly. "Marcus, I have a confession to make."

"What, are you guilty of highway robbery as well as housebreaking?" he said, a laugh in his voice.

"Do be serious for a moment!"

"It's hard to be serious in a situation such as this." Catching her indignant glance, he made the gesture of a fencer acknowledging a hit, folded his hands in his lap and made his mouth prim.

She choked back a gurgle of laughter. "The portrait – it's not the original," she said, watching his face.

"Not the original," he repeated faintly, eyes widening.

"It's a copy. I painted it." She rushed on, her words coming out as a tumbled, disjointed speech, "My widowed father is a man who has lived mainly on his wits. Over the years he has turned his hand to various schemes in attempts to make money, none of which have been particularly successful. Oh, don't misunderstand me – Papa is not a criminal – but his methods of transacting business can be a little, well, unorthodox. I have always loved painting and often painted original pictures for him to sell, allowing him to present them as his own work. Women who paint for anything but pleasure are frowned upon, you know, and it would not have done for anyone to know that I was the artist. My paintings provided a steady income, far better than his madcap schemes that often came to nothing. Then, some months ago, he discovered that I been secretly copying famous paintings purely for the fun of it. He was astonished and delighted at their quality—"

"I'm not surprised!"

"Well, I don't like to boast, but my efforts are passable."

"Passable! My good girl, your talents are extraordinary! But I interrupted you - please continue."

"Papa became unwell and was unable to work. His creditors began pursuing him forcefully. Matters grew more desperate than I knew. These circumstances, and his concern for me, led him to take a foolish step." Leonora dragged in a steadying breath. "One day I returned to the attic room where I paint to find that my copy of The Virtuous Courtesan had disappeared. I confronted Papa and eventually he confessed that he had taken it. Worse still, he admitted that he had sold it *as an original.* Horrified, I begged him to give me all the details so I might redress the situation. Realising he had gone too far, he was contrite and told me that he had sold the painting to the Earl of Allingham, who owned a great estate called Rookery End in Surrey. Papa was too ill to do anything, so I sent him to stay with his brother in Vienna while I began planning to retrieve the painting. The only solution I could think of that would not embroil us in scandal, or put us in prison for fraudulent dealing, was to steal it. A-And so... and so, I came here tonight to do just that."

"When you were caught by me," he said softly.

Unable to speak, she gave an almost imperceptible nod. He was looking down at her, a hint of laughter and something more, something indefinable in his eyes. Her heart turned over in her chest. A thrill of pleasure shot through her as his hand cupped her face, and he brushed his thumb across her cheek.

"Leonora, I care little for paintings, original or otherwise, but I can appreciate true beauty and grace when it appears at dead of night in my library. I don't want to let you out of my sight again. It sounds madness, but all the months and years I've spent searching for love seemed to have been distilled into this one night. Into you."

"You can't mean it," she said, feeling a little dazed.

"I do. You're all I've ever wanted or dreamed of. Don't ask me how I know, but I do. I'm not wealthy - all I have to offer is a love that lasts forever – but my heart, if you want it, is yours. Would it displease you to receive my addresses?"

"To – to –? Oh!" She gasped and then swallowed. "N-No, it would not displease me," she admitted, "but I feel I ought to say something sensible such as it being too soon. This is the first time we have met!"

"I knew the instant I set eyes on you," he said simply.

"Did you?" she replied, blushing and torn between tears and laughter. She covered his hand still cupping her face with her own. "I confess I did too and now I feel foolish."

"Why?"

"Because I've never believed in love at first sight."

"Neither did I." He took her in his arms. "I've waited so long for love and now I've received my leveller at last – from a housebreaker. Our addle-brained fathers created this mess, but, given how things have turned out, we should thank them and seal our future in a much more civilised way."

With that, he lowered his head and kissed her.

***

Much later, Leonora raised her head from his shoulder. The candles had long since burnt down and fingers of dawn light were stealing into the room. A becoming flush tinted her cheeks, her eyes sparkled and a smile played about her lips, and even an undiscerning observer would have noted she looked like a woman who had been thoroughly kissed. As indeed she was.

"Marcus," she murmured.

His head was leant against the back of the chaise longue and his eyes were closed, but the arm he had about her tightened. "Hmm?"

"Has your headache gone now?'

"Strangely enough, it has," he said, flashing a knowing, utterly satisfied grin.

Her blush deepened. "And are your pockets really to let?"

"I'm afraid so," he admitted. "Does that alter things?"

"Not in the slightest. I still want to marry you as soon as it can be arranged."

He chuckled. "Thank God for that, my adorable little housebreaker! Somehow we'll restore the fortunes of the House of

Allingham together, albeit without the help of The Virtuous Courtesan."

"There is something else you should know," murmured Leonora, unable to repress a giggle, her gaze on the opposite wall.

He opened his eyes and turned his head to look at her. "What's that, darling?"

"That painting. . ."

"Which one?"

"The one over the fireplace."

"You mean the miserable looking fellow in Tudor armour?" he whispered, leaning closer, his lips caressing the sensitive skin beneath her ear. "Awful, isn't it?"

She sighed with pleasure. "Oh, it has some merit - I've just noticed it's an original by Titian and worth a fortune."

The End.

Phillipa Ashley

Phillipa Ashley read English at Oxford University before working as a freelance copywriter and journalist. She is the author of five romantic novels including Decent Exposure, which won the RNA New Writers Award 2007 and was adapted into a Lifetime movie called Twelve Men of Christmas. She lives in a Staffordshire village with her husband and daughter.

Also by Phillipa Ashley:

Decent Exposure

Wish You Were Here

Just Say Yes

It Should Have Been Me

Fever Cure

Feast of Stefan

A blast of icy air rippled the skin on Nick's forearms as the stranger flung back the pub door.

"I am so sorry; I make you all have the goose bumps."

Smiling, the stranger stamped his boots on the mat, snow melting off the toes onto the quarry tiled floor. They were shiny knee-high leather, with square toes. He wore a black woollen overcoat, so long that the hem almost brushed the tiles and he had thick black hair curling past the top of his collarless shirt. Add the sharp Slavonic cheekbones and the accent and it could only mean one thing.

"Russian," muttered Amos Harding over the rim of his pint.

"Polish," murmured a lady by the fruit machine.

"Slovakian," said the stranger with a warm smile. "My name is Stefan Grzwoski. How do you do?"

His dark eyes swept the room, a glance that took only a few seconds but seemed to focus on every individual, checking them out one by one.

A strange sensation glowed in the centre of Nick's chest as Stefan's eyes rested on him. Nick wasn't entirely sure it was a pleasant feeling but everyone else around him seemed to be smiling as if they'd just received a refund from the taxman. Even old Amos was grinning; not the prettiest sight considering he'd lost most of his teeth a good few years before.

As for Sarah...a moment ago, she'd been sitting next to Nick, laughing at one of his jokes. Now, she was staring at Stefan, her lips parted like a little girl who'd just opened the door on Christmas morning and found a pile of presents under the tree – with Santa still there.

Icy fingers skittered up Nick's spine as Stefan's gaze lingered a little longer on Sarah than anyone else in the pub.

Nick didn't blame him.

Sarah was easily the prettiest woman in the village and Nick would have had words with anyone who'd said otherwise. She had beautiful green eyes; bouncy auburn hair and skin sprinkled with pale freckles that made Nick want to kiss each one. She also had glorious breasts and a fantastic bottom. Nick wouldn't have been honest if he didn't admit to that.

Of course, Sarah had no idea how he felt about her eyes or her freckles or her bottom. She had no idea that Nick had been in love with her for the past year.

No one in Hatherton knew the agony he'd been through, seeing her almost every day and never finding the right moment to tell her how he felt. Tonight, he'd finally plucked up the courage to buy her a drink and had been just about to ask her out when this exotic character had walked into the pub.

Stefan clapped his hands together. "So, does anyone want a drink? It is the least I can do, now I have made you all cold." His deep, full-blooded chuckle rang around the pub and the Woolpack erupted into life again.

Nick laughed too. As if this Stefan could have any effect on his chances with Sarah. The man was a complete stranger, there was no reason to see him as a rival, no reason even to talk to him.

As Stefan handed over a wad of notes to Aggie, the landlady at the bar, locals emerged from the snug and the lounge now word had got round that free drinks were on offer.

Stefan's arrival might be a very good thing. While the locals were all distracted, he could get on with the task in hand: plucking up the courage to ask Sarah out.

His ex, Fiona, had been gone from his life for over two years but Nick had tried and failed to rejoin the 'market,' as his mates termed it. Beyond having lunch with his sister's mate (who had clearly been doing him a favour) and an evening of speed dating that had been more excruciating than a night in the celebrity jungle, he'd refused all attempts to lure him out on a date.

There had always been Sarah, filling his mind and obliterating all other women. He'd worried he was becoming obsessed; her face, voice and scent filled his mind from the second he woke, as he drove to work, and even sometimes in the middle of a meeting.

Take tonight - he'd only ended up buying her a drink by chance. He'd been playing a game of pool when she'd walked into the Woolpack and sat down in the corner, checking her mobile, obviously waiting for a friend. Nick had gone through agonies, wondering if that friend might be male or female. Half an hour later, she'd disappeared, leaving left her coat on her chair. He guessed she'd gone to make a call in the corridor and sure enough, she was soon back in the bar, a frown on her face.

"Everything all right?" he asked as she passed him.

"Yes, I mean, no. That is, there's nothing serious but Catriona's had to cry off. Her youngest boy has chickenpox."

Nick was glad Sarah couldn't see his inner grin of delight. "Oh dear, that's a shame. Can I get you a drink, after all?"

"Well, if you've finished your game. Yes, why not?"

He resisted punching the air in the middle of the Woolpack, and contented himself with strolling (when he really felt like running) to the bar.

Aggie, the landlady, handed over a white wine and a pint. "'Bout time you two got together. Sarah's locked herself away long enough, poor lamb. It's been over a year now hasn't it?"

Aggie was right, of course, it was high time Nick made a move. It had been over eighteen months since Sarah's husband had been killed in a car accident, leaving her a widow just short of her thirtieth birthday.

"A year and eight months. Or thereabouts,"said Nick, his heart sinking in case Sarah overheard. "And it's only a drink with a friend, Aggie. Don't you get choosing a hat for the wedding."

"As if. But you shouldn't be a hermit either, Nick. We're all getting worried you might have taken a vow. All you seem to do is live at that factory or play pool in here all night."

Aggie wasn't quite accurate. In winter, Nick also trained with the rugby club and in the summer months, he played cricket for the village team. That's where he'd first met Sarah. He'd been in the same club as her husband, Robbie, and while they hadn't exactly been mates, he'd liked the man. Bloody good spin bowler too. Nick smiled at the memory of Robbie skittling a rival team one balmy August evening. Afterwards, he'd celebrated with the rest of the team and their supporters in the cricket club pavilion. He'd thought Sarah was attractive but, knowing her even less well than her husband, he'd barely exchanged more than a few words with her.

Nick swallowed hard as he caught sight of Sarah watching him from the other side of the bar. Was that how the village saw him these days, a lonely workaholic bachelor?

Was that how Sarah saw him?

"Keep the change, Aggie," he said, winking as if to show he knew what he was doing. Yet as he carried the drinks back, he could hardly bear the schoolboy thumping of his heart or the way his mouth seemed to have turned to sandpaper.

He'd spent such a long time, waiting for Sarah to be ready. He'd gone to Robbie's funeral, of course. Over two hundred people had packed into the tiny church. Nick had crammed into a pew at the back, one of the many men who were staring ahead, trying not to empathise too closely with Robbie's family, who were weeping openly and not caring who saw them.

Already, he realised now, he must have been fond of Sarah but at the time, he'd told himself he only felt a natural human sympathy for her.

But not long after the funeral, when she'd popped into the pub to thank Aggie for the wake, he'd stopped avoiding her eyes.

He'd nodded, then smiled, then passed the time of day and asked her how she was – God, that was a daft thing to do considering her husband had just died. She'd smiled and answered: 'you know' – which he didn't, but she hadn't made him feel uncomfortable or stupid, even though any words he could offer had been trite.

Perhaps that was when he first fell for her.

But even when he'd realised he was in love with her, it had been far too soon to ask her out. He had no right to crash in on her grieving. But tonight, before Stefan had arrived, he'd resolved that this was the time when he would finally do it. Any moment now, he would find the courage to say: "Sarah would you like to go for dinner?"

"Here you are. One white wine, at least that was what it claimed on the bottle," he said, handing her the glass.

Butterflies took flight in his stomach as she smiled her gratitude. "Thanks, Nick, I needed this."

It was all he could do not to take her in his arms and kiss her, there and then in the middle of the pub, and sod Amos and his mates and anyone else in the world.

"Hello. I hope I not interrupt you. I come to introduce myself."

Sarah's lips parted again in that girlish smile of delight and Nick turned round.

Stefan towered above them, his hand thrust out. "It is Nick Maynard, no?"

The hairs prickled on the back of his neck. "Yes, it is. How did you know that?"

"My engineering business in Slovakia is planning to buy your company's new electronic control system and I come to find out how it works before we install and commission it. Your managing director did not tell you?"

Nick had a vague recollection of his boss mentioning that his firm would be getting a visit from Eastern European clients some time soon, but the details must have escaped him. Besides, he had other things on his mind.

"Yes, of course," he said, grasping Stefan's hand.

The man had a grip like a grizzly and it was all Nick could do to keep the friendly smile on his face as Stefan almost crushed his bones. If this was some display of phallic competition, Nick suspected Stefan was playing hardball.

"And who is this lady?" asked Stefan, his eyes sparkling with the flickering reflections of the Woolpack's fire.

"This is Sarah Yelland, a friend of mine."

"Sarah. Hello." Stefan gave a formal little bow that Nick thought was cheesy but Sarah must have found charming because she smiled broadly and even started to blush. Nick's hopes ebbed away like snowmelt over Hatherton Falls.

"A great pleasure to meet you both," said Stefan, settling his tall and rangy frame on the bench next to Sarah. "What good fortune that I see you on my first night in the village. I think we are all going to have a good time here, no?"

***

After the first moment of universal generosity, Stefan settled into the normal routine of the Woolpack. Over the next few weeks, he did everything right. He bought his fair share of rounds and lost a respectable number of darts matches. He appeared willing to listen to endless debates about rugby, cricket, sheep, European subsidies, walkers, weather and traffic. He told the odd joke, listened to everyone else's and even seemed to get most of them – and take things in good part when he didn't. He helped Aggie behind the bar when two of her staff cried off sick, got Jago Myers' ancient car to start and even gave Amos a lift to the betting shop.

"I wouldn't kick him out of bed," said Aggie dreamily on a rare night when Stefan wasn't in the pub.

"He's all right for a furriner," said Amos.

As far as Amos was concerned, that meant Stefan was practically a saint.

Over the next few weeks, Nick saw Stefan most days at the factory. Several evenings a week, when Nick wasn't training, they met at the pub. Sarah was there more and more often, sometimes with Catriona but often alone, as if she was waiting for Nick.

Or rather, he realised, waiting for Stefan...

The weirdest thing was that Nick often hoped Stefan would walk in too, and that was a hope he couldn't understand. When Stefan was around, the confusion of feelings made him feel dizzy. There was jealousy, of course, and then guilt for begrudging Sarah's obvious delight in Stefan's company. There was despair that he was losing her and most disturbing of all, there was pleasure.

Nick couldn't for the life of him think why he enjoyed being with Stefan so much, for the man was surely stealing away the woman he loved in front of his very eyes. Yet he couldn't deny or suppress the happiness that enveloped him when Stefan was around or wish away the disturbing glow in his chest.

Sometimes, Nick almost hated Stefan but other times, it was if he was mesmerized too. He wondered if Stefan had slipped something in his pints...

One evening, when they were all sitting round a table by the fire, Sarah asked the question Nick had been longing to but was too professional, polite and afraid.

She leaned forward, twirling a strand of her hair around a finger, and asked. "So, Stefan, how much longer are you staying in Hatherton?"

Stefan looked deep into her eyes, in a way that would have been creepy from other men but seemed completely natural for him.

"I'm not sure, Sarah. It seems to be taking longer than I expected. I have a lot to learn, eh, Nick?"

"He's doing fine," said Nick, trying to cling onto some hurt and anger amid the tide of painful pleasure squeezing his chest. "The system will be ready to ship to Stefan's Slovakian factory soon so he can return to his home."

"I am in no hurry. I am enjoying my work here more than I ever expected."

"Won't your family be missing you?" asked Sarah.

Stefan gave a mock sigh. "Unfortunately, I live alone so there is no one to miss me. The castle is a big place for one man."

Her eyes were like dinner plates. "A castle?"

"It is called a castle but perhaps it is more like a house, a fortified house. With a moat."

"And a drawbridge?" asked Nick, sarcasm finally breaking free of the honeyed fug that had enveloped him.

"Indeed. But it does not raise and lower any more. The mechanism rusted years ago but perhaps, Nick, your company can replace it? Maybe one of your motorised systems can get it started again?"

Sarah's eyes shone in delight. "Oh yes, Nick. You must try. I'm sure you could work something out."

"You should come to Slovakia to see it," said Stefan.

Nick replaced his pint carefully on the table. "I'm just off to the gents."

"Have one for me, mate," Stefan said, imitating Nick's Derbyshire accent to a T.

Sarah let out a giggle and because the imitation was so uncanny and unexpected, Nick couldn't help laughing too. He trotted off to the gents with a grin on his face that made both his jaw and heart hurt. As he opened the door to the corridor, he risked a glance back at the table where Stefan was regaling the bar as if he had been born in the village. It was as if he was one of them; as if he had become Nick, or a luxury, glamorous, supercharged version.

As he splashed water on his face, Nick forced himself to look in the mirror. He was pale after a Peak District winter and badly in need of a haircut. At least there was plenty of hair and no grey yet thanks to the Maynard genes. He kept himself fit and tried to keep his intake of after-match pints to a reasonable level. He was over six feet, sturdy and strong. He liked to think he was reasonably good looking, he hoped Sarah thought so, but compared with Stefan's extraordinary looks, he knew he was a very ordinary mortal indeed.

What woman wouldn't fall at the man's feet?

Back in the bar, Sarah and Stefan were laughing away like old friends. Nick lifted his chin up and fixed on his best matey smile. He had his pride but inside he felt that his heart was being removed, slowly and secretly - and that no glow, however seductive and powerful, could fill the void.

***

"You're going home?"

Nick had to ask Stefan to repeat himself, he was so amazed. It had only been a few days since he'd last drunk with Sarah and Stefan in the pub, and now the man had announced he was leaving Hatherton.

"Yes, I return to Slovakia very soon. My job here is over."

"But...you haven't said anything at work."

Stefan smiled pleasantly. "I think I have seen all I need to, but before I leave, I would like to have a party."

"Are you buying the drinks?" Amos piped up.

Stefan grinned. "Of course, and we will have food if Aggie will oblige? I think we should call it The Feast of Stefan."

Laughter rippled round the bar and glasses were raised.

"No problem," said Aggie, clearly delighted to have the business.

Nick stared into his pint, dumbfounded. There had been no hint at work, no word from his boss that their Slovakian client was about to return but Nick wasn't going to look a gift horse in the mouth. Stefan was leaving, that was all he needed to know.

Relief, heady and powerful, flowed through his veins followed by dismay as he realised Sarah would probably be devastated.

Unless, of course, she decided to follow Stefan to his castle.

***

Nick kept out of The Woolpack for the rest of the week but there was no way he could avoid the party. It would have been unprofessional and spineless to stay away and he owed it to Sarah to turn up. She'd expect it and broken-hearted though he was, Nick couldn't bear to have Sarah think he was a coward.

At nine o'clock, he dragged himself off his sofa and up the hill towards the bright lights of the pub, like a moth drawn to the flame. The sky was clear, pinpricked with stars and a full moon lit up the hills, a light frost glittering on the trees and fields.

He had to shoulder his way through to the bar past locals who were slapping each other on the back and raising their glasses in toasts. Someone turned on the sound system and a party tune blasted out. Aggie was behind the bar, happily dishing out drinks at Stefan's expense, but there was no sign of Sarah.

"She is late," said Stefan, suddenly appearing at Nick's side.

"I know. It's not like her. I thought she'd be one of the first to arrive."

Stefan put a hand on his shoulder. "Maybe she has a date."

His skin prickled where Stefan had touched it. "I joke," said Stefan, with a grin. "Don't worry, she won't miss this party."

Nick slipped outside to ring Sarah on his mobile and as he shouldered his way back into the bar, the noise hit him like a sledgehammer. Every single person from the village must be in there.

"You have called her?" Stefan shouted down his ear.

"Yes, but I got her answer phone."

"What about her mobile?"

"Same."

Stefan's breath was hot against Nick's cheek. "Perhaps the battery is flat?"

"Maybe. I'm sure she's fine, but if she tried to get the car out she might have run into some trouble. The roads are pretty icy but even so, she should be here by now, whether she walked or took the car."

Stefan patted his arm. "I think we should go to her house and see if she is okay."

Nick shook his head. "No, I'll go."

Stefan gripped Nick's arm tightly. "I will come with you. I was a mountain guide in Slovakia before I started my business. It's not a good idea to go out alone in these conditions."

Nick set his jaw, his eyes watering with pain as Stefan's powerful fingers dug into his bicep. "It's not that bad."

"I think you are mistaken, Nick."

The pain in Nick's arm melted away as Stefan released it and lifted the curtain away from the tiny window next to the pub door. Outsized snowflakes whirled against the panes. The hubbub of the party quietened and Nick heard the wind howling around the stone building and snow battering the tin lid of the Woolpack's log store.

It was impossible. That amount of snow couldn't have fallen in such a short time! There had been hardly a flake on the ground when he'd gone out to use his mobile.

He glanced back at the pub to express his astonishment but all around him, the partygoers were drinking and laughing, oblivious to the blizzard raging outside.

"So I come with you," said Stefan slowly.

Nick nodded. "I suppose it wouldn't be bad idea," he heard himself say.

Stefan clapped his hands together. "Good. Then we go."

Grabbing his coat from a chair, Nick followed him out into a black and white storm.

"You are okay?" called Stefan, stopping to slap Nick on the back, sending him staggering forward.

"F-fine." Nick's teeth chattered and he blinked. Stefan was wearing only the T-shirt he'd had on in the pub .

He smiled. "Come, Nick, I go first and you follow behind."

Nick tried to protest, saying he knew the way to the cottage but the gale snatched his breath away. His cheeks and chin began to grow numb and snowflakes stung his eyes. Within minutes, he could barely see Stefan even a few paces ahead, the man's broad back was just a dark blur. Lowering his head, Nick battled with the wind, struggling to lift his feet above the deep drifts, the heavy denim material of his jeans already soaked through.

Soon, Stefan had disappeared from view entirely; the only evidence he had existed were his deep footprints stretching ahead in the snow. Nick barely had the energy to wonder what had happened to him; his brain seemed to have turned to slush. Even his limbs weren't getting signals to move and every step felt like he was climbing a mountain in leaden boots.

It was only a mile, he told himself, only a mile...and Sarah was at the end of it.

A faint light twinkled ahead. Sarah's cottage. It had to be.

As he dragged himself along, planting his feet in Stefan's footprints, the light grew closer. Suddenly he was pushing at the cottage gate, opening it just enough to struggle through and stumble along the path, a wild flurry of sleet battering his face.

As he reached the porch, his legs slipped from under him and he fell, banging his head on something sharp. He touched his scalp and felt moisture, warm and thick. The snow turned pink in front of his eyes.

"Sarah!"

The snow danced in a wild frenzy of white and then he knew no more.

***

"Nick? Nick...Nick!"

He opened his eyes to see Sarah's face. His hand was gripped tight in hers, her face anxious.

"Sarah?"

"Are you okay? You slipped in the snow and hit your head on the door-scraper."

He touched his head, feeling not the cold hardness of the icy doorstep but the softness of Sarah's sofa and the warmth of her wood fire against his face.

"You must have passed out. I managed to get you into the sitting room. Nick, you are heavy!"

"Thanks," he winced as his fingers found a lump on his scalp.

"You've got a cut. It's not bad but I think you should go to hospital to get it checked out, although how we'll get you there in this snow, I have no idea. I can't believe how it came down so suddenly. One moment I was in the shower and the next, I looked out of the window and it was piling against the fence. I didn't dare come out."

"What about Stefan?" asked Nick, still feeling fuzzy.

She frowned. "What about him?"

"He came with me to see if you were okay. When you didn't turn up to the party we were worried."

She kept her eyes on his hand and stroked his thumb. "I...wasn't going to come. I wanted to come but you see, tonight would have been Robbie's thirty-fifth birthday. I thought I couldn't face it but then...I changed my mind. I jumped in the shower to start to get ready, and then I heard such a racket outside and found you out cold on my doorstep."

"Oh, Christ. Robbie's birthday? I'm sorry, Sarah."

She let out a brief sigh then smiled. "Yes, but I decided I really wanted to see you."

"See me?"

She swallowed and he felt the pressure of her fingers as they closed around his hand. "Yes, you, Nick. Really."

He pushed himself up against the sofa arm and winced. "But what about Stefan? He's still out there. I have to go and find him, make sure he's okay."

Gently, Sarah pushed his shoulders down. "You really have had a bang on the head. You must have concussion. Stefan didn't come with you. He phoned, he's at the pub."

"No. He was with me. He went ahead. He said he was a mountain guide..."

"Right, that's it! I'm phoning for the air ambulance if I have to. You really must have concussion."

Nick opened his mouth, shut it again and meekly settled back against the cushion. "Perhaps I do just need a rest. So Stefan phoned?"

She didn't look convinced but answered him anyway. "Well, Aggie did, actually. She had a message from Stefan for you. He says you told him you were going to come to the cottage and fetch me but he didn't want to miss the rest of the party and disappoint everyone so he turned back. "He said," she smiled wryly, "he knew you'd be safe with me."

Nick's head throbbed. Maybe, when his brain cleared, he'd be able to make sense of what had happened. Or maybe he wouldn't.

Maybe he didn't want to.

Sarah's voice was soft. "Nick, I've been waiting for you to ask me out for quite a while now but you never said anything. At first I thought it was too soon after Robbie for me to want to start seeing another man. Then I realised you thought it was too soon and so we've gone on, dancing around each other until I wanted to scream."

He didn't trust what he was hearing. It was too dangerous a fantasy.

"But what about Stefan? I thought you and him..."

Sarah shook her head. "Oh God, no. I mean, he's gorgeous of course. Almost too gorgeous to be human, if you know what I mean, but there's something about him...I just can't take him seriously as a, well, a potential date. No, Stefan's more like a cousin or an older brother or...I don't know. There's just something peculiar about him." She held his hand tighter. "Nick, can we please not talk about him? Now I've got you on your own and we're actually speaking, can we just..."

Nick reached for her and before she could finish, she was in his arms and he was kissing her. Her mouth tasted so sweet and welcoming and if he'd thought that Stefan gave him a glow, it was nothing to the glorious heat that filled him now. Sarah's eyes shone with desire and happiness and Nick knew that Christmas, his birthday and England winning the World Cup and the Ashes had all come at once.

"Nick," she whispered as he ran a finger down her neck, stopping at her cleavage.

"Yes, Sarah."

"I don't think you're fit to walk back home."

He felt light headed and at the same time, overcome by a feeling that was much more earthy and sensual. "No. I think you're right. I'm behaving inappropriately which is a sure sign of a head injury."

"It is, and I think you should stay here."

"I'm not going to argue," said Nick. "I'd better do exactly as you say."

Much later, as Sarah led him up the twisting cottage stairs to her bedroom, Nick glanced out of the window. His jaw should have dropped. The moon was full and there was just a light covering of snow now, an icing sugar dusting of the dale - but definitely no deep drifts or blizzards. He could even make out the lights of The Woolpack gleaming at the edge of the village.

He wasn't surprised and silently thanked Stefan. The man might not a saint but he wasn't such a bad bloke after all.

The End.

A Bolt From The Blue

"Oh, don't be such a pensioner, Lisa! It's not as if we're going up Everest!"

My friend Carolyn had a face redder than the morning sky that had greeted us as we'd crawled out of our two-woman tent that morning.

"But do you really think Converses are the ideal choice for climbing up a mountain?" I asked.

She rubbed her mauve suede gloves together. "Yes, I do. Now, it's a lovely day, the sun's shining. Let's get going."

She was right. It was a lovely day, white clouds sailing across a pale blue sky and very mild for mid October. It was the first day of our 'girls only' camping weekend in the Lake District. I needed a break after my fiancé, Finn and I had gone our separate ways a few months before.

Hmm. Separate ways.

The truth was that Finn had gone his separate way – from me. I'd been happy with our relationship. I thought I'd been happy, anyway, and only found out how far apart we really were when I'd gone to pick him up from his physiotherapists one evening. She'd 'been good enough to fit him in after hours', he'd said, because his coccyx was giving him some trouble. I'd caught them shagging on her treatment table and then gone slightly berserk with a medical lamp. Those ultrasound machines are pretty pricey, I'm told, but funnily enough Ms Physio didn't complain.

The criminal damage was the start of an 'orgy of recklessness' (according to Finn) that had led to the camping weekend. I know camping doesn't sound that reckless, but I needed to get as far away from Finn as possible, in every way – and given my budget after the split, the Lake District was at the limit of my means.

I went along with Finn's story that we'd parted by mutual consent, because I'd thought it was better to leave with dignity than face the gasps of shock and pity that would inevitably follow. Besides, he'd always liked things tidy: our loft flat in North London had been so pared back and minimal, my mum thought we'd been burgled. Inside, things weren't so neat. My heart had been as jagged as if Finn had taken a hunting knife to it.

So Carolyn, my boss and friend, had agreed to come along on the expedition.

Carolyn clutched the thighs of her skinny white jeans as we rested on one of the rare 'flat' sections of the rocky path.

"We could have stayed in a nice spa hotel instead of camping," she said between gasps.

I collapsed against a boulder. "I've been there and done that with Finn. He'd have hated this. If a place didn't have five stars and 110% approval on Trip Advisor, he wasn't interested."

"But camping? Hiking?"

"You said it wasn't Everest..."

"I changed my mind, my God, I'm actually sweating - and look at my hair!"

Carolyn was turning a bit Marge Simpson but I knew better than to insult my boss. "You look like a cover model. You always do. Look, we can reach that little tarn up there and break out the flapjacks."

"Lisa, I know you think you've got something to prove to Finn but this is ridiculous."

"No. I've got something to prove to myself."

She sighed. "In that case, I still say that roughing it in the Lake District in the middle of autumn is cutting off your nose to spite your face. Oh fuck, look at that!" She pointed to the path that lay ahead; a crazy staircase hacked into a dizzyingly steep rock face. "When we slip and break our necks, you'll have the satisfaction of knowing it was all for Finn's benefit."

"Ha ha. Very funny."

An hour later, neither of us was laughing. Carolyn was lying on her back whimpering while I dialled 999 and trying not to stare at her ankle. Not even her personal Pilates trainer could have helped her get her foot in that position.

Covering Carolyn with my coat, I wiped the drizzle from her face as the sky turned leaden.

My words tumbled down the phone. "Mountain rescue. As quick as you can."

In no time, the fellside was swarming with people in red jackets and Carolyn was hooked up to a drip by a tiny woman who turned out to be the team doctor. The air was filled with the deafening chop chop of rotor blades as a yellow helicopter descended.

Despite the happy juice filling her veins, her face was white with pain. I held her hand, squeezing back a tear and called into her ear. "I'll be at the hospital as soon as I can."

Her nails dug into my wrist. "Aren't you coming with me?"

"Can I go with her?" I shouted.

A man mountain with a jaw line hewn from granite took me aside. "There's no room. The helo's got to pick up another casualty in the next valley," he shouted. I thought he added something about keeping the weight down but the rotors were too loud.

"I'm sorry, Caro. I'll have to follow in the car. Looks like I'll have to stay with Hagar the Horrible."

Hagar bent down beside her, patted her arm and then helped the team carry her to the helicopter. I hugged myself, hoping the downwash wouldn't sweep me off the fellside.

A minute later the silence was eerie and it was as if Carolyn had never existed. I broke the news to her parents, trying to reassure her father that she'd be okay. It was difficult to hear him, what with her mum screaming in the background.

Clicking off my phone, I took a deep breath as radios crackled around me and the tiny woman called everyone to her. "We've got another shout," she told her team. "Elderly man with a suspected fractured wrist in Bannerdale. It's all hands to the pump."

While they packed up the kit in double quick time, I sat on a rock, hugging my knees, feeling like a spare willy in a nunnery.

"Bye!" they called cheerily and disappeared off into the mist.

That left me and Hagar, the man mountain in Gore-Tex. He was a foot taller than me with a pair of very impressive hiking boots. Finn had been tallish and very lean, of course, from all those dawn aerobics classes but his feet had always worried me. Mum had told me never to trust a man with small ones and for once, she'd been right.

I clapped my hand over my mouth to stifle a giggle.

"I'll be okay to get down on my own," I said, wondering what Hagar looked like without the hat and days' worth of stubble. I half expected him to rip off the beanie and shake out his hair like Cat Deeley in the L'Oreal ads. Swishssshh.

This time my laugh escaped and echoed over the fellside.

Hagar frowned, his ice blue eyes watching me intently. "Are you sure you're alright?"

"Delayed shock," I said, swallowing hard. "Got any Kendal mint cake?"

The corners of his mouth quirked in a smile. "Can't stand the stuff, myself. We'll be in the car park soon. There's an ice cream van there so you can get a Cornetto."

Raindrops fatter than blueberries started to splash down as we walked off the fell. All the way down I tried to make conversation. How busy were they? Did they get annoyed with people for calling them out? Wasn't it nice weather for the time of year?

Half the time he didn't seem to hear, which was hardly surprising with the beanie hat and the cagoule hood. The other half, he responded with a mix of grunt and monosyllable. Maybe he knew I didn't really need a reply and that the shock of the accident had given me verbal diarrhoea.

"Aren't you supposed to be cheery, sardonic and offer me reassurance?" I mumbled as the car park came in sight.

He turned. "Did you say something?"

"Know any jokes?" I asked.

"Only the one about the woman who tried to climb a mountain in Converses."

Suddenly in the car park, my legs felt wobbly. Relief at reaching terra firma was eclipsed by anxiety for Carolyn.

I dashed for my car but Hagar caught me up. "Wait a minute. I'll get an update on your friend." He spoke into the radio and nodded. "Carolyn's safely at the hospital being assessed but she'll be fine. There's no point you breaking your neck racing after her. Take your time."

He fetched a cup of tea from a van in the car park and produced a slightly fluff-covered Mars bar from his Land Rover. As we stood by the car, burning our tongues on the tea, Hagar pulled off his hat. There was no swish but he did have something in common with Cat Deeley; thick dark blond hair streaked with toffee highlights that hadn't come out of a packet. There was definitely Viking blood in those veins. I ran through a list of possible names for him, most involving strapping Nordic gods.

Sven, Erik, Thor, Beowulf...

It was no good; I couldn't banish 'Hagar' from my mind. I blew hard on my tea as he caught me watching him, and he rubbed a hand over his head, startling his hair into life.

"Where are you staying?" he asked through a steamy tea cloud.

"Dale Bottom Campsite."

He chuckled and distant thunder grumbled. Surely that was a coincidence?

"It should be interesting down there," he said. "It beats me why they sited a camping field at the bottom of that dale. It always floods and there's a storm coming on."

"I gathered that by the cloud thingy up there."

He nodded towards the west, still bright with late afternoon sun and then pointed east where the sky was as swollen and bruised as Carolyn's ankle. When he scratched his stubbled chin, I half expected sparks to fly. "Mind you, I like a good storm myself. The light's always intriguing and the cloud formations are beautiful...but I must be on my way. We'll get another update on your friend but let us know how she gets on after that."

You mean come round to the base with a donation, I thought, but treated him to my best brave girl smile. "I will."

He slammed the tailgate of the Land Rover as I rummaged for my car keys in back pack.

"Thanks for your help," I said. "You know, all the time we've been exchanging witty banter, you haven't told me your name."

All I saw was his Land Rover rumbling out of the car park.

***

Her fractured ankle pinned, Carolyn was kept in hospital for a couple of days before her parents arrived to take her home. I went back to the campsite, packed up the tent and loaded into the car. Then I headed for the mountain rescue base and sheepishly, handed over a cheque for two hundred pounds.

"Wow," said the doctor, raising her eyebrows. "Not everyone bothers to say thanks and this is a lot of money."

My cheeks heated up with shame. The call out must have cost ten times that and the volunteer team did this job for nothing. "Carolyn's mum and dad insisted on the cheque. We're going to organise a fundraising day at work to raise some more money for you."

The doctor smiled. "Great. We need everything we can get."

I noticed her glancing at her watch. I should walk away. Really. But the words gushed out of my mouth. "Um... that guy. The one who walked me down. I mean he didn't actually walk me down and hold my hand or anything... but he came with me while you all went to the next shout."

"Oh...you must mean Hagar."

"Really?"

Her mouth twitched and her eyes twinkled. "Just our little joke."

Oh shit. He had heard me then, even above the rotor noise and he'd told everyone else.

She laughed. "He's at work today. At the Studio by the Bridge House."

***

Funnily enough, I had to walk past the Studio on the way to the village car park. The tiny stone and slate building was tacked on the end of a row of shops and galleries. The window was packed with pictures, watercolours, oils and postcards. A few were a bit twee or garish for my taste but some were genuinely beautiful. I had a sudden urge for a souvenir.

I pushed open the door and the bell dinged. There was a counter and cash till but no sign of life apart from some kind of jazz drifting from a smaller room at the back. Lingering in the main gallery, I admired the paintings, stopping in front of one or two, wondering which to buy.

The music stopped and footsteps rang out on the slate floor. "Hello."

Hagar stood there, holding a framed painting. He wore a pair of jeans, ripped at the knee with tawny hair just visible through the tears. His ancient sweater was spattered with paint.

He smiled, slowly and warmly and a thunderbolt hit me. Wham.

"I went by the base," I said as his eyebrows knitted together in puzzlement. "They said you worked here. That's...nice," I pointed to the picture in his arms. It was a pastel, the kind of thing Finn would have called 'modern' aka weird. The scene was clearly the fell side, instantly recognisable from our incident, half bathed in light, and half deep in stormy shadow.

"It looks like a Julian Heaton Cooper," I said, hoping he wouldn't be offended at the comparison. "I've got one of his prints in my bedroom."

He laughed softly. "I wish. My stuff's not fit for Julian to wipe his feet on, but thanks for the compliment. Are you an artist?"

"Graphic designer. Carolyn runs an ad agency but I'm no art connoisseur. Oh, I didn't mean that yours isn't very good..."

You could almost hear the whirr of me back pedalling, but Hagar's eyes were amused.

He rested his painting on the counter. "Would you like a cup of tea?"

"I don't want to interrupt. I just want to say thank you from me and Carolyn. I thought you'd like to know she's gone home with her parents. They say she'll be okay with some rest and physio."

"That's great and there's no need to worry about interrupting me," he said, his smile now rueful. "The light's gone now and I can't work. I'll put the kettle on. Come through to the back."

He lit the flame on an old ring and dumped a kettle on it. He sat next to me on a battered futon, the only piece of furniture in the room that wasn't covered by canvasses, paint, brushes and boards. We talked about the paintings, both his and the other artists whose work was on show in the gallery.

"Did you get a soaking at Dale Bottom?" he asked, watching me over the rim of his mug.

"Not much." I lied, tingling in all kinds of places. The truth was I'd had to pack the dripping tent away and even now it was mouldering in the back of the car. I'd have to re-pitch it in my yard when I got home, if it would fit.

He placed his mug on the slate floor. "Look. I'm sorry about yesterday. I was probably a bit...brusque. I shouldn't have taken my problems to work but my divorce came through that morning."

I cradled my mug and held my breath as he went on.

"Bloody stupid really. It's been a couple of years now since Debbie and I split up; there are no kids which I suppose is a blessing. It's all amicable, all...fine, apart from her leaving me for a winch man from the RAF, that is. I didn't think I'd bother about a piece of paper after all that but it hit me like a sledge-hammer, that final letter." He let out a sharp breath. "But I ought to shut up; you won't know what I'm talking about."

I put down my mug. "Oh, I think I have an idea."

"Really?"

"Yes. Except that my partner ran off with his physio. Or rather he hobbled off with her. He had a bad back, you see."

I decided to leave out the part about the lamp and the ul-trasound.

Hagar got to his feet, opened the cupboard above the sink, and pulled out a bottle of Laphroaig.

"Whisky?" he asked.

I thought of the damp tent, of my two-hour car park ticket and of the last time I'd wanted to do something this much. I couldn't remember.

"This early?"

"Well, we've both had a shock."

As he collected the mug from my hand, his knuckles brushed my hand. There was a tightness in my throat, a mix of fear and uncertainty that was spreading to my chest and through my limbs. He went through to the shop and I heard the bolts being drawn and the 'closed' sign being turned to the outside world.

My heart started to thud, like the slow whop whop of the helicopter blades as he poured the Laphroaig into the mugs and raised his. "Slainte. To the joy of going separate ways"

***

They tell you that discussing ex-partners isn't the best way to go about engaging with someone new; and that relationships formed in traumatic situations don't last.

In our defence, we didn't talk about Finn or his wife for long before the space between us had narrowed to nothing. He put his arms around me and his tongue slid into my mouth, and mine into his. He tasted of whisky of course, and I didn't mind the stubble one bit.

Hours later, we lay on the futon under an old tartan blanket, the dark blue twilight washing through the bare windows of the studio. My toes brushed against one of the stacked canvasses. His arm was under my head and my breasts were pressed against his chest.

The clock chimed six and I lifted my head sharply, bumping his chin. "Oh, bugger."

He frowned. "What's the matter?"

"I think I've just got ticketed on the car park."

He chuckled again. "So what?"

"I'll get a fine."

"And?"

"I...I don't do things like that. Ignore parking tickets. Break the speed limit. Go on camping weekends..."

"And sleep with strange men called Hagar?"

My cheeks heated up. "I suppose it's too late to worry about the car park, isn't it?"

His eyes were laughing at me, but in a good way and he pulled me closer to him, the warmth of his body melting my resolve. I settled against him as his hand curved round my bottom.

"Relax," he said. "I know the warden. I'll sort it out. Say you were on emergency work."

"Tomorrow then, first thing I'll move it..."

A brief pause, punctuated by my breathing.

"You'll be going home, then?" he asked.

"Yes, I am. I was. I have a few days left off work."

He looked down at me from his green eyes. "It's a start. More whisky?"

"Maybe later?"

The blanket slithered to the floor. I felt his breath against my chest as he lowered his head to kiss me. "You still haven't asked my real name, Lisa..."

I lifted my head and closed my eyes, anticipating another thunderbolt. "No."

No need to ask.

All around us, and on me, in gentle, confident brush strokes, was his signature.

The End.

Also from escapewithabook.com

Midsummer Eve at Rookery End by Elizabeth Hanbury

One Midsummer Eve, three Regency love stories......

Midsummer Eve is the traditional time for love divination, when gentlemen and ladies can hope to meet their true love. Lord and Lady Allingham hold a lavish ball every year at their country estate, Rookery End, for the Regency ton to celebrate this custom. Amid this romantic setting, six people are about to fall in love...

Love Engineered by Jenna Dawlish

Louise Thomas, owner of a large estate in Devon is ready to fall in love, but only if she can find a man who will put up with her thirst for knowledge in the engineering and scientific world.

Charles Lucas is one of the country's top Engineer's, tipped to be the new Brunel. He is too busy with his work for love – especially with a member of the gentry. When he meets Louise, she interests and intrigues him like no woman before. But he must make some serious decisions when he hears disturbing rumours about her.

Sprig of Thyme by Jenna Dawlish

England, 1853. Jilted five years ago by a man masquerading as a tutor, Adella believes she has come to terms with her loss. She has moved on with her life, no longer a governess, she is happy in Bath helping her brother, a doctor. That same man moves to Bath under his true identity; a rich landowner. Fate throws them together and she discovers the secret behind his betrayal. Can she live with the consequences it holds for both of them? Can she learn to forgive him?

Pursued by Love by Georgia Hill

When a modern day Darcy and Elizabeth are stranded in a snowbound inn, they're forced to re-evaluate their first impressions of each other ...

From the moment Perdita Wyndham meets Nick Wainwright she thinks he's the most arrogant man she's ever met. It's appropriate then, that he's playing Darcy in his company's production of Pride and Prejudice! But acting opposite, in the role of Elizabeth, Perdita can't deny that Nick is also the most intriguing man she's met in a long time.

In a Class of His Own by Georgia Hill

Forsaking the bright lights of London, Nicky Hathaway comes to live and teach in a sleepy Herefordshire town. She's expecting the quiet life but then Jack Thorpe takes over as her headmaster...

Nicky is a woman who won't take no for an answer and soon all sorts of sparks are flying between her and the implacable but gorgeous Jack. But, is it hate or love that's growing between them? And just what is Jack's big secret?

Nanny Behaving Badly by Judy Jarvie

Strong, silent-type single dad hires wild streak nanny—off-limits opposites attract. Maddie Adams hopes for a smooth ride in her new temporary coffee shop job so she doesn't mean to make the worst impression possible with the handsome café owner, Lyle Sutherland. His suggestion that she becomes his son's replacement nanny shocks them both. Hormones are on fast-track living at close quarters. When attraction and passion are unleashed between boss and sassy super nanny, Lyle's secrets and a shock pregnancy challenge old wounds. Can a new baby unite their futures? Can fledgling love survive corroded trust?

Off Limits Lover by Judy Jarvie

Anya Fraser and Max Calder are both medical professionals who spend their work time caring for others. In their private lives they struggle with the past. Anya has a debilitating fear of heights. Max loves parachuting. He takes chances, she wants life to be slower, safer to protect herself and her son Callum. Max is willing to take a chance on the attraction they both feel. Can Anya get past her fears after she's already lost one partner with a dangerous lifestyle?

Lightning Source UK Ltd.
Milton Keynes UK
UKOW031043110112

185159UK00001B/10/P